Kama Kahani

The Thief of Poompuhar

Kama Kahani

The Thief of Poompuhar

Nila Iyer

Penguin metro reads

An imprint of Penguin Random House

METRO READS

USA | Canada | UK | Ireland | Australia
New Zealand | India | South Africa | China | Singapore

Metro Reads is part of the Penguin Random House group of companies whose addresses can be found at global.penguinrandomhouse.com

Published by Penguin Random House India Pvt. Ltd
4th Floor, Capital Tower 1, MG Road,
Gurugram 122 002, Haryana, India

Penguin Random House India

First published by Random House India 2010
This edition published in Metro Reads by Penguin Random House India 2020

10 9 8 7 6 5 4 3 2

ISBN 9788184001129

Typeset in Sabon by InoSoft Systems, Noida

Printed at Repro India Limited

www.penguin.co.in

FSC www.fsc.org MIX Paper from responsible sources FSC® C047271

This is a legitimate digitally printed version of the book and therefore might not have certain extra finishing on the cover.

For my grandfather who loved telling stories
and my husband who loves to hear them

PROLOGUE

The moonlight shone like a champakam flower in spring. A waft of air floated across the river, turned into a breeze, and sang its own lullaby. Twilight had disappeared reluctantly; and the inky purple sky with its single shimmery adornment captivated the tall, slender girl who stood by the river Kaveri with her head tilted upwards.

Mekalai was no ordinary girl. It seemed as though fire coursed through her veins instead of blood. Her beauty was like a star—ethereal, unbelievable, and forever. She seemed to belong in the sky, not on earth. Perfectly sculpted, with honey-tinged skin; large, smouldering eyes with charcoal-dusted eyelashes; a sharp nose; and a full, sensuous mouth, her allure was enhanced by an inviting mole just below her lower lip. It was rumoured that a mad poet from Madurai had written odes in praise of her exquisite beauty.

The moon blinked at her sleepily. Mekalai smiled back, her knee-length raven-coloured tresses billowing like clouds in the night breeze. 'Please look after me,' she silently shot up a prayer. The moon glowed back reassuringly. Manikottai, the fortress in which she had spent all seventeen years of her life, stood at the edge of the bustling port town of Poompuhar. Towering over the landscape like a large dark monster, it almost disturbed the tranquillity of the night. The fortress seemed to cast a dark spell over everything around it. It looked eerily evil, portending gloom. Mekalai gazed at it intently. There was a strange gleam in her eyes. 'It won't happen,' she muttered. 'I won't let it happen.'

She turned around and bolted like a comet towards the dark, disappearing into the sepulchral woods. Mekalai moved like the wind, her feet barely touching the springy, dew-drenched grass that stretched out for miles like a velveteen carpet studded with diamonds. Flowers sparkled like stars in the sky, their fragrance forming a heady cocktail for the senses. The woods unfurled, deep, mysterious, and intriguing. But Mekalai knew her way around. Just as she knew what she was looking for. Ever since she was seven, she had frequented these woods, running wild, climbing trees with the boys, and setting off on solitary adventures.

She stopped by an abandoned ringed well. There were many like this around the banks of the river, on the fringes of the woods that no one ever really wanted to enter. The only people who dared to set foot inside these were thieves, fugitives, or smugglers. But Mekalai was none of these. She was just a young girl with secrets, secrets that she held close to her troubled heart.

Mekalai let herself down the well by the rusty shaft

and pulled out something wedged between the ancient damp bricks. It glistened brilliantly in the moonlight. Her sword. Her iron companion, her secret confidante, her force. She looked at the exquisitely crafted gold handle, with a band of amethyst and sapphires embedded around the base. It was said that a great courageous Velir chieftain had once owned this sword. Over time, it had passed through several hands and finally after decades, landed with her family. And it was her brother who had gifted her this family heirloom. She let out a deep sigh and curled her slender fingers around it...

The night stood silent witness as she practised her craft. It was like a dance, a dance between Mekalai and her nightly companion. The curved sword made lithe, light moves in the air and her graceful figure swayed along with it. Her smoky eyes were incandescent in the night, as if a common soul ran through her sword and her, igniting a fire in her.

She must have practised for an hour or more when she noticed a sudden movement. The stillness of the night had been disturbed as the rustling in the undergrowth seemed to draw closer and closer. A faint sound echoed from the depths of the tall banyan, mango, palmyra, and neem trees. She instinctively drew the sword behind her. No, it wouldn't bode well for her to be seen with it. A woman with a sword? In the land of Narasimhan? This was unheard of and the news would spread like wildfire. Mekalai hid behind a tree and closed her eyes, praying that it was just some wild animal. Just then, the movement ceased, as abruptly as it had started. Mekalai stood as still as she could. 'Must have been a rabbit,' she thought, her breath quickening. She wasted no more time, climbed down the shaft, and hid her sword in its original place.

The moon seemed to conspire with her as it simultaneously retired behind the clouds. Mekalai made her way back through the woods, into the town and to her home, pondering on her narrow escape. As an expert swordswoman, she had nothing to fear except the discovery of her identity.

Poompuhar glistened in the moonlight. She made her way through the perfectly aligned streets with their torched lamp posts that cast dancing shadows on the walls. She passed the tall buildings, the warehouses that held various kinds of merchandise, and the famous street known for its bales of silk, all up for sale. She wound her way through the towering mansions speckled with night lamps on their top floors.

A few horses and some stray dogs looked at her curiously, but luckily no people were in sight. Poompuhar was a town that slept well. The solitary guard outside her home was deep in slumber, his grunting snores assuring her that she was unnoticed. She crossed the cold grey stone steps and entered the house. The gleaming mansion, with its buttery-white plastered walls and ornate carvings, had been built by her father. The door was imposing, made of wood and iron and crowned by an arch of intricate murals. The elaborate patio had beautiful life-size mayilvilakkus strewn around, throwing their flickering light on everything around. As she let herself into her expansive chamber, her maid stirred. But she didn't wake up. Mekalai went to her window and stared at the sky above. The moon was back in its full glory...

CHAPTER ONE

MEKALAI AWOKE AT SUNRISE to the sound of rhythmic chants from the nearby Murugan temple. The incessant ringing of the conch shells could be heard from a distance. It reminded her of the childhood stories her father used to tell her—of the priests who were so gifted and powerful that their combined chants used to bring the rain gods themselves to their doorstep. He had then given her a small conch shell as a way for her to call for him if she ever wanted him. Smiling at the memory, she stretched her long limbs and sat up. Her bed was huge; four people could have slept in it easily. The head was made of ivory and had intricate carvings of peacocks. The bedding was made of soft, downy swan feathers, a luxury only the very affluent could afford. But Mekalai had never considered herself wealthy. For her, wealth did not matter as much as the legacy that needed to be preserved and respected.

She remembered her father's indulgence and her mother's wrath. 'You are letting her get out of control,' her mother would chide her father. 'She might as well have been born a boy. See how she runs wild all the time. Just yesterday, the next-door neighbour was here with enough complaints to fill the king's coffers. She not only broke into their house and painted a moustache on that old hag there, but also broke their new swing.'

Her affable father would only chuckle indulgently, letting his wife do all the worrying. He also knew part of Mekalai's tomboyishness stemmed from the way she worshipped her older brother. Nithilan was swashbuckling and popular even at twelve, and little Mekalai wanted to copy him in everything, much to her mother's chagrin and her father's amusement. She ran with the boys, sometimes outrunning all of them, and was an undefeated champion in catapulting. She was usually the first to climb up to the top of the mango tree with its golden juicy fruit. Mekalai often went off alone through the gritty lanes where the affluent never set foot, pausing at the little stalls with their colourful dolls and terracotta animals. She walked along the river banks, picking the wildest flowers and arranging them in large brass urns all around the house. Her mother would be appalled that such lowly flora had found its way into their stately home and would promptly throw it all out.

Mekalai's parents had always emphasized the importance of being self-sufficient. The children had learned this lesson well, but many around them attributed their natural self-reliance to the riches that they possessed. Mekalai, however, knew that wasn't true. Behind all the gold and the opulence, there lay in the hearts of her brother and herself a profound sadness that no amount of wealth could take away. Just then, the sound of her maid, Guna, bringing her cardamom-flavoured milk in her silver cup, shook Mekalai out of her reverie.

'I didn't realize you would be awake already,' Guna said in response to Mekalai's smile.

Mekalai reached for the silver cup and said, 'I love the music of the town awakening. It somehow fills me with hope.' She took a long sip from the cup and replaced it on the tray. The maid withdrew silently, leaving her mistress to her thoughts.

Mekalai walked to the window. Far below she could see the merchant town of Poompuhar come alive. She saw the fishermen with their straw baskets on their heads, filled with the lustrous unmoving catch of the day. Vendor women with containers of sweetmeats and steaming hot rice cakes called out loudly to one another. The lanes wound down to the town square where the merchants sat with their wares. While some had their own shops, the others merely set up stalls on the roadside. Anything you wished for and could dream of this side of the Vindhyas was available in Poompuhar. Marupakkam, the other side of the town, was where the affluent lived and Patinapakkam bustled with the cries of merchants, fishermen, and other traders. Verdant orchards with riotous blossoms and a number of gardens such as Uyanam, Uverivanam, Kaverivanam, and others, dotted the city. Lush mango trees stood along the lanes, and children clad in imported silks ran around playing with their wooden dolls. The women showed off their husbands' prosperity with aplomb, sporting large diamonds, rubies, and emeralds. The men of Poompuhar, largely traders, merchants, and court officials, had a swagger to their walk, thanks to flourishing overseas trade and connections. Most of them had mistresses whom they housed generously in mansions only slightly smaller than the ones in which they lived themselves with their wives and children. Gambling dens dotted the city, away from the main town square, in the little side lanes frequented only by fishermen and vendors. These dens stayed open all through the day, to cater to the addicts, not even shutting down at dawn. In tandem, the numerous taverns, which sold liquor from all over the country, did roaring business. It was not unusual to see a businessman surreptitiously make his way into one of the taverns, having gained a windfall.

Far beyond, on the seashore, catamarans of all sizes floated alongside bigger boats and ships. These ships entered the port without slacking sail and brought the yavanas, the foreigners, from Rome, Greece, and Egypt. The foreigners were of utmost interest to the young women of Poompuhar. They were intrigued by their beauty, and were convinced that these were Gandharvas who had descended on earth. The yavanas, in turn, expressed their interest in the exotic beauty of these girls and what ensued was mostly harmless flirting under the watchful eyes of the fishermen.

Leaning out over the ledge of her bedroom window, Mekalai was unaware of the interested, furtive glances her unadorned beauty was attracting from the passers-by below. It was unusual to see a young woman of an obviously affluent family being so unselfconscious of the sun's rays, and rarer still to see one stand in appreciation of the heat rather than hide from its burning powers. This was Mekalai's favourite time of the day. While the darkness of the night was her ally, the light of the morning brought her newfound joy and hope.

Just then, outside her mansion, Mekalai spotted the potter Ilango, shaping beautiful little urns with that indescribable grace that only he possessed. She remembered how, as a child, she would run past the guards and into his little thatched shed, and ask to play with the wheel. He would happily let her. Her nanny would invariably drag her away, her little hands smeared with clay.

Mekalai remembered how her mother had lamented in vain because no matter how hard she tried to mould her daughter into the sedate, shy, and demure woman she needed to be to find the right matrimonial match, her husband seemed just as happy to let Mekalai grow into her real personality. 'If she is to be wild, then so be it. I will not rein her in, for what is the beauty of a stallion when it is chained to the barn door?' Her mother would go away mumbling about what the neighbours were saying already, as her father twirled Mekalai around, making her laugh out joyously.

The years had passed in bliss and scant worry for anything but when Mekalai's father fell prey to conniving rivals, his once flourishing diamond business started to dwindle. At first, there were just a few losses, but soon, like vultures rounding up at the smell of fresh kill, competitors saw their opportunity and forged alliances against him, seeking to undercut his business. The ruthless machinations of those he had considered his partners and friends broke his spirit.

His frequent visits to the taverns to drown his sorrows in toddy only worsened the situation. Finally one day, he was found dead on the staircase clutching his heart, his eyes wide open. Mekalai was heartbroken and clung to her mother in grief. What she didn't realize, until it was too late, was that with the passing of her father, something broke inside her mother too. She was devastated and became uncaring and unconcerned about anything around her. Her condition grew worse with every passing day until finally, six months later, she too passed away, leaving ten-year-old Mekalai and sixteen-year-old Nithilan to fend for themselves. Nithilan instinctively rose to the challenge of being Mekalai's guardian. He was resilient, determined, and fiercely protective of his sister. Their father had amassed enough wealth to support the next ten generations and the youngsters never saw worry due to financial reasons. The thorn in their side came in the form of their maternal uncle Komagan.

Komagan was wayward, good-for-nothing, and got by mainly with the wealth his father had left him. He was known to have disreputable connections and had always been extremely jealous of Mekalai's father. Seeing both parents dead, he now staked claim to the family's property.

He and his wife Chudarmani had three spiteful and extremely spoilt children. Keeran was the oldest, an obnoxious child with a penchant for hurting small animals in sport; Nithya and Nakeeran, twins born a few minutes apart, insisted on doing everything together, and that included tormenting Mekalai. Once when Mekalai, still only seven, had gone to Keeran and begged him to tell his sisters to stop, he had laughed cruelly at her and pushed her into a pit full of fire ants. Miraculously, Nithilan had unexpectedly arrived on the scene, hearing her cries, and had rescued her. In the fight that had ensued between Keeran and Nithilan, Nithilan had drawn the first blood, an insult Keeran had never forgotten or recovered from. However, with the passing of their parents, Komagan had again started to insinuate himself into their home and their lives, to the extent of proclaiming that Keeran should marry Mekalai. Keeran, now much older, was as famous for his opium excesses as his unwavering penchant for nautch girls. Consequently, Nithilan had told his uncle in no uncertain terms that it was a match that would never be. Komagan had not imagined that his move would be thwarted and he was furious. Over the years he had tried every trick in the book to usurp the mansion and its precious belongings, but with little success.

Even though they now had only each other, Nithilan and Mekalai were happy and content with their lives. At first, both of them had maintained a stoic silence about their parents' demise. But one day, when he returned from his lessons at the ashram, Nithilan had found Mekalai crying quietly while looking at the peacock comb her father had got for her. Nithilan had wiped away her tears and twirled her around just like their father used to. Laughing and crying, they had both shared their sorrow with each other, trying to come to terms with the loss. By spending all his time with her, he had ensured that she become the strong, happy child she had earlier been. Looking back at that time, Mekalai realized how much and how soon her brother had had to grow up, to make sure that she had a longer childhood. As the years went by, their bond had grown deeper, held together by their love for each other and the thread of common sorrow. The promise of a happy future which they would welcome together strengthened this bond of the brother and the sister.

But now, Nithilan was gone...it was like a dark cloud that hung over her life. Her sibling, her only friend and family, had disappeared. All because of Narasimhan. Her eyes darkened with anger and then brimmed with tears. She fought them back furiously as she heard Guna entering her chamber. Guna gently reminded her that it was time for her bath as she had to go to her friend's wedding. They made their way to her private bathing block, behind her mansion where the Kaveri flowed in all its glory. As she climbed down the dank granite steps into the cool water, the universe seemed to fade away...

CHAPTER TWO

MEKALAI PADDLED AROUND IN the water for a while and when Guna arrived with a paste of turmeric, sandalwood, and gram flour, she climbed up the steps again. She let her maid anoint her with the paste. Her thoughts were somewhere far away, her eyes wistful.

'If I may speak, sweet mistress,' said the young girl, 'you look troubled.'

Mekalai looked at her and wondered whether to share her thoughts with her.

'Talking helps,' said the girl gently.

Mekalai slid back into the water, not wanting the young girl to see her sudden tears. How could she explain the depth of her sorrow and her feeling of helplessness which she usually kept tucked away behind her mask of control, her only defence against those who waited by the sidelines, watching for the first sign of weakness from her?

Guna stood on the steps for a minute and then walked away. Mekalai came out of the water and wiped her body with the simple cotton cloth that was laid out on the steps. As she sat on the last step, her feet in the water, she heard the melodious notes of the flute. She knew that her modesty was safe, as there was no way for anyone to look into her private bathing area, but the lilting music brought upon her a sudden craving for company. Tiny little fish swam around, occasionally nibbling at her toes and she smiled at their play. 'If only I could forget my cares and be able to play,' she thought to herself. The only time she ever truly forgot her worries was in the dead of the night, when there were no spectators. She longed for her sword, the sword her brother Nithilan had presented her. Nithilan who was missing...

Her mind raced back to the day he disappeared. It had seemed a normal day like any other. She was on her way to the Murugan temple with him. 'You look so beautiful, Mekalai...one of these days, some prince is going to come and whisk you off,' he had said. She had laughed, feeling unusually shy. It must have been her laughter that caught *his* eye...Narasimhan's evil eye, she thought.

Narasimhan was the chieftain of Poompuhar. His face showed his forceful nature, with its strong, cruel features. In fact, he may have once been handsome, but years of debauchery had left their imprint on his face, making it look cold and bloated. Narasimhan owed his allegiance to the Pandya king and went to the court at Korkai at regular intervals to mark his loyalty and comradeship. Tamilakkam was a splendid state with the Cholas, Pandyas, and the Cheras reigning supreme. This was AD 225, towards the turn of the third century. The king was too engrossed in his foreign trade connections to be bothered about much else. The Pandya splendour was fading and the king was weak. Narasimhan took full advantage of this fact and ruled the land with a vice-like grip. His tyranny had become legendary. He forcibly took land, lives, and women. Nothing was safe under his vicious reign. No one spoke openly of his oppression and cruelty for fear of being executed.

Narasimhan was a clever operator; he covered his tracks well. He had built for himself the Manikottai fortress, a formidable structure that covered his sins from public view. He had grown almost complacent about the practically powerless monarch at the helm who had chosen to turn a deaf ear to the rumours of Narasimhan's tyranny. As Narasimhan rode through the shaded lanes of the city that fateful day, he ruefully reflected that his current mistress had lost her charm. He had abducted her from Thanjavur on the day of her wedding. Now three months later, she suddenly seemed used and old. He ran his mind through the dancing girls in his harem and the devadasis at the temple but none of them excited him. Narasimhan liked his mistresses to be beautiful, not just attractive or pretty. He possessed everything—wealth, power, a strong bastion—but not an enviable mistress. For his everyday needs he could make do with just about any girl but his mistress had to be special, extraordinary.

The roads of Poompuhar truly seemed paved with gold, as the glittering dust sparkled in the sun. And as he rode through this alley of the land, so tormented with his mistress situation, he saw *her.*

Mekalai was bent over a little calf, feeding it tiny bunches of grass. She stroked the animal and whispered gently into its ears while it nuzzled her lovingly. The moment Narasimhan set his eyes on Mekalai, he knew he had to have her. She was more stunning than any girl he had ever ravaged. He scanned her lithe, full figure that was scarcely hidden by the wispy robes she wore while she was lost in her own world, oblivious of the impact she'd had on the tyrannical chieftain. As the wind blew Mekalai's way, her upper robe lifted and he caught a glimpse of her generous breasts. He took in her full lips, the perfectly shaped black mole just beneath her lower lip, her impossibly tiny waist, and her graceful hips. Almost instinctively, he was filled with unbridled lust. This girl would be his mistress.

He surged forward and brought his horse to a thundering halt right in front of her, blocking her way. Mekalai looked up in surprise. He looked at her in a way that defiled her, and her expression slowly turned to disgust. She tried to make her way past the horses and henchmen, with her brother hovering protectively close when Narasimhan got off the horse. Towering ominously over her, he blocked her way, as if daring her to go past him. 'Get on the horse,' he commanded.

Mekalai stood rooted to the spot, her gaze unwaveringly defiant. She felt no fear towards this obnoxious oppressor, just a deep loathing and a sense of revulsion.

Aghast at her disobedience, Narasimhan got off the horse and walked towards her menacingly. By now, the scene had generated quite a lot of interest and people were watching furtively from the sidelines. The citizens of Poompuhar looked on, dumbstruck with fear, not daring to utter even a word. They pretended not to look, hustling and bustling around, but they all knew that Narasimhan was in his element that day. Meanwhile, Narasimhan inched closer to Mekalai. He grabbed her arm and roared, 'Come with me now! How dare you ignore my command?'

That's when Nithilan, his eyes flickering with violent anger, came forward and said, 'Sir, leave my sister alone. You have to let us pass...'

Narasimhan turned to the young man, ablaze with fury. It was an unwritten rule in Poompuhar that no one told Narasimhan what to do, let alone defied him. As he turned towards Nithilan, there was something in his eye that stopped Narasimhan—a dangerous glint that told him to keep off. Also, Nithilan was the best swordsman in and around the kingdom and the news of his skill had reached Narasimhan's ears. He had never lost a duel.

Narasimhan was fully aware of the fact that his henchmen would stand no chance if Nithilan decided to fight. The guards had closed in on both of them when Nithilan drew his sword. Narasimhan let out a short laugh. With a slight motion of his hand, he ordered his men to step back. Nithilan put the sword back into its hilt, took his sister's hand and walked away. As she left the spot, Mekalai could feel Narasimhan's eyes burning into her. She knew that this was not over and the worst was yet to come...

The next day when Nithilan and Mekalai were whiling away their time, playing chess, they were interrupted by the sudden arrival of Narasimhan's henchmen. What had initially seemed like a peaceful afternoon now turned into a fierce battle. Nithilan made sure that Mekalai hid in the storeroom while he tried to fight Narasimhan's men. He held them off for some time but he was grossly outnumbered and he knew it. With a neat, leopard-like jump out of the window, Nithilan fled deep into the woods and was never heard of or seen again. But even if he was gone, he had left behind a legacy for his sister: the secret training he had given her on moonlit nights. There was scarcely any man who could wield the sword better than Nithilan. And if there was anyone who could match him, it was his sister...

A year earlier, on her sixteenth birthday, Nithilan had planned a special gift for his sister. Mekalai had grown into a stunning beauty, and Nithilan who by now was matched by none in sword fighting, worried for her safety during the times that he was away. So on her birthday he had decided to spring a surprise.

'Where is my gift, beloved brother?' she had asked playfully, expecting yet another diamond necklace or anklet but instead, he placed a long, gleaming sword in her hands.

'These are not safe times, Mekalai,' he had said. 'I want you to be self-reliant.'

And so her lessons had commenced. They practised in secret on the terrace of their home at night, so no one would discover them. Under the translucent light of the moon, Mekalai came alive, the spirit of her sword charging through her blood. Impressed by her enthusiasm and intelligence, her brother didn't treat her like a woman who was inferior, but rather as an equal. Nothing was too strenuous or too difficult for her. He taught her the finer points of fencing, defence, and parrying, even showing her how to read her opponent's mind by his body language. He told her that alertness was everything in a duel. The mightiest had lost their duels and their lives due to a second of distraction. Mekalai drank everything in. While Nithilan was a hard taskmaster, Mekalai was a persistent and a quick learner, so it wasn't long before she actually struck down his sword in a duel. Just six months into her training, Nithilan was spreadeagled on the ground and her sword playfully touched his chest.

'What next, mace fighting?' he had teasingly ribbed her.

The truth was that Mekalai loved sword fighting. She took to it as naturally as a bird takes to the sky.

She loved the sword, carefully picked out from their treasured coffers by Nithilan, just for her.

'I hope I find a match just as perfect for you,' he had laughingly said one day and Mekalai too had burst into laughter. That laughter still rang in her ears as she sat there lost in the past, the silent river the sole witness to her sorrow.

Later that morning, she reluctantly began getting dressed for her friend Sandana's wedding. She chose bright yellow and blue robes lined with shimmering jarigai. Her face was untouched by makeup save for her eyes, which she generously lined with kajal. She left her hair loose, even though she knew it was frowned upon. Guna had run camphor and sandalwood fumes through her tresses that morning after her bath. Mekalai placed her mother's rakkodi on the crown of her head, where it shone like a solitary red sun. Her anklets were of diamonds and pearls and they made a tinkling noise as she walked. Guna drew a little intricate bindi on her forehead. Mekalai usually hated wearing earrings but today, she put on a pair, beautiful orbs of rubies and emeralds designed in traditional temple jewellery style. Before she left the house, Guna insisted on performing the ritual of warding off evil.

Mekalai clicked her tongue in exasperation. 'I am getting late, Guna. Trust me, I can ward off evil on my own.' The young maid, who was used to her mistress's ways simply waved the chillies and salt around her and then ran to throw them in the fire, where they burst into flames.

'See, see, mistress, they say that when the chillies burst into flames it means people have cast their evil eye on you,' she exclaimed.

Mekalai shrugged. 'That's really up to them, isn't it? I can take care of myself. Don't worry.' And with that she turned and walked out of the house. Old men who played dice under the shade of banyan trees lifted their watery eyes to get a glimpse of her. The lane leading to her friend Sandana's house was lined with shops that sold everything, from the choicest of silks and velvet to precious stones, ornaments, exotic perfumes from abroad, and much more. She could see merchants of all shapes, sizes, and ages craning their heads to get a good look at her.

As she passed a particularly opulent jewellery shop, its owner stepped out blocking her way. This was Selvan, about fifty years old. He had successfully outlived two wives both of whom had died in childbirth. Now he was actively looking for the third.

'Listen to me, Mekalai,' he gushed breathlessly. Mekalai, who was about to pass by ignoring him, stopped wearily. This wasn't the first time that Selvan would be proposing to her; he had done it twenty times in the past, to no avail. She shot him down mercilessly each time but it was evident he wouldn't take no for an answer. Starting the conversation like they were already in the middle of it, he said impatiently, 'You have no one. I have no one...we could take care of each other.'

The other merchants waited with bated breath for her icy response. This was the most fun part of the day and they waited eagerly for it.

'You have six children,' she retorted.

Some of the merchants sniggered loudly. Selvan shot them a dirty glance and continued, a ghastly smile pasted on his face.

'Heheheh, that's true. And my poor children need a mother,' he gushed on. 'Not that you would have to take any trouble. I will employ enough nannies. You will live like a queen; I will cover you in gold and diamonds. You're good, kind...err...beautiful... Don't waste more time, Mekalai. Be mine.'

'No, thank you,' she said almost rudely and walked on before he could utter another word.

Ever since her parents had died, all the neighbours did was wonder whom she would marry. Who would give her away? Proposals for marriage had started coming in from the time Mekalai was twelve and an angry Nithilan would boot the suitors out of the house. She was too young and vulnerable he thought, and he didn't wish to marry off his beloved sister just yet. Now she was seventeen, and it was the merchants of Poompuhar who sought her ardently. Unfortunately, even though they were many in number, most of them were too old, too fat, or too oily for her. The incessant proposals from these merchants had become a daily occurrence, which exasperated Mekalai. Just because they thought she was orphaned and helpless...

The wedding pandal was brightly lit with brass

and silver lamps, and flower decorations filled every nook and corner of the house. Little birds made out of the long coconut palm leaves hung about everywhere while colourful kolams of impossibly intricate designs decorated the floor. Copper pitchers of munneer stood on various tables. The stronger liquids were being served in the antechambers inside, for the men. Bottles of foreign liquor too stood around for those with sophisticated tastes. The tables groaned under the weight of all the food put out on them. Sweetmeats of every possible sort had been laid out, including sweetened squares made of ghee, jaggery, and flour; flat succulent paniyarams, fluffy appams that looked like perfect snowflakes; and ven pongal. Huge trays of imported dry fruit were passed around.

Mekalai made her way through the milling crowd to find her friend. Sandana was going to wed a silk merchant from Kanchipuram. Her unimaginably handsome dowry was much talked about and a record that looked like it wouldn't be broken in a long time. Her father was a prosperous diamond merchant and her wedding jewellery alone would fill five large chests. In addition to that she would take with her a thousand cows, a hundred elephants, twenty thousand gold ingots and a specially crafted gold statue of Lord Murugan with a spear encrusted with real gems. Wherever she turned, Mekalai could only hear people avidly discussing the dowry.

Seeing that her friend was surrounded by a motley crew of aunts and other relatives who would all ask

Mekalai the same question—'When will we see you in wedding finery?'—Mekalai made a quick exit. She found her other friends in an antechamber, avidly discussing the prospects outside.

'That one,' said Lakshmi, 'in the blue dhoti, well, he is an accountant in the king's court. Now if only I could catch his eye...'

Arul, in the meantime, was engaged in an avid discussion about the shape of the earth.

'I am telling you,' she said animatedly, 'they have just discovered that the earth is in fact round in shape. Someone in Greece...'

'How boring,' reflected one of the girls. 'I shall continue to believe that the earth is flat and it is propped by four unbelievably huge elephants...'

'And I am confident that one of those elephants just walked into the room,' said Arul softly. All eyes turned in the direction she was looking at.

'Uh oh,' she murmured. 'This is that fatso. His mother is bride-hunting for him. But no one wants to marry him, do they now?'

Adiban, who had just stuffed four enormous laddoos in his mouth, sadly only seemed to reinforce her opinion. His size was alarming and dressed in gaudy silk, he looked like a giant, overstuffed bolster.

'Run,' urged one of the girls, 'there comes his mother.'

The brood scuttled away, except Mekalai, who really couldn't care less. The lady's beady eyes glinted at Mekalai like a vulture's. Mekalai glared back.

'My son will inherit five thousand acres of land when he turns thirty. There is also the abundant family wealth. You can't even imagine how much it's worth. I could buy all of Poompuhar if I wished,' she said pompously.

The son, who was so gloriously sitting on a magnificent inheritance and his ample bottom, had let the laddoo spill out of his mouth. His belly convulsed spasmodically as though egging him to eat more. Mekalai could see that her companions were watching from afar, unable to suppress their giggles.

'He has also lost some weight, you know,' the lady continued, but not without casting a doubtful glance towards her laddoo-stuffed son. All of his six chins quivered.

'So...will you?' asked the lady. 'It is the opportunity of a lifetime.'

Adiban suddenly hoisted himself up and stood there, blinking at them.

'I am sure it is,' said Mekalai sweetly. 'But I have to decline. He doesn't match the rest of my furniture.' And with that, she turned on her heel and walked towards her friends, leaving both mother and son gaping.

The heavily incensed air inside the pandal gave Mekalai a slight headache and the interested glances of all the men only made her even more cross. Within the next half an hour, she had thwarted six more attempts at marriage proposals by overenthusiastic pot-bellied merchants and found herself wishing increasingly that she was elsewhere. After Arul had done a thorough survey of the place and had proclaimed that there was not a decent man in sight, her friends had possibly fled to one of the inner rooms to avoid similar proposals. She wondered if she could just leave without anyone noticing. Her friends now caught up with her, looking utterly bored.

'Not a decent man in sight...' sighed Arul.

'Really, is that all you girls think about?' asked Mekalai.

'Just because you are not normal doesn't mean others are as retarded,' shot back Lakshmi. 'I intend to marry before the harvest season is over and that's that.'

'Maybe if you stop thinking so much about marriage, it will happen sooner,' said Mekalai seriously.

'Oh please, Mekalai,' wailed Arul. 'Here you are warding off proposals by the minute and having odes written by mad poets in praise of your beauty, and here we are trying to get just a little bit of attention... you don't talk!'

'Well,' said Mekalai rolling her eyes, 'please feel free to take any of my ardent admirers...'

'Ooh,' said Arul suddenly, sitting up as though she had been stung by a bee. 'Look at that one. Girls, I'm going for the kill...'

The prey in question was a handsome man who unfortunately looked like he was harbouring a rather unpleasant smell under his nose.

'He looks snooty as hell,' muttered Mekalai. 'It's like butter won't melt in his mouth.'

'Tsk tsk,' her friend said. 'Please make yourself scarce so we won't have to wilt under unrealistic comparisons and have a fair chance.'

Mekalai rose to leave but by then the young man was already in front of her. She heard both Arul and Lakshmi swear under their breaths.

He didn't even glance in their direction, concentrating all his attention on the divine damsel he had just set his eyes on.

It turned out that he was a minister at the king's court and had come down to Poompuhar on an official visit. He was new in town and didn't know anyone, at least not anyone interesting. So he enquired if she would be kind enough to take him around.

Mekalai could sense that her friends were waiting with bated breath for her reaction, and she smiled graciously.

'That is very kind of you, sir, but unfortunately I tend to be very busy. I have to respectfully decline your offer.'

The man looked completely taken aback. Clearly, he had no experience in facing rejection. Mekalai studied his face briefly. True, he was handsome but he did not really appeal to her. His eyes were set too close together and his mouth had a snobbish, domineering twist to it.

As they watched the man turn and walk away, clearly perplexed by his sudden failure to impress, Arul said, 'Congratulations, Mekalai. You have done it again. A handsome suitor comes along and you flick him away carelessly. Really, you should get your head examined,' she finished strongly.

Mekalai took no notice of them and wandered away.

It was then that she noticed her cousin Keeran and uncle Komagan making their way towards her. It was too late to hide, so she stood there, trying to look civil if not friendly. How she wished she could disappear. Her uncle made no attempt to look pleased either.

'I see you have left your hair loose like a wanton woman,' he sniggered.

Keeran leered. She noticed that his glance went directly from her face to her chest and lingered there. Automatically, she adjusted her robes and with a voice soaked in sarcasm, said, 'Yes, Uncle, I do try to live up to your expectations.' And she turned to leave.

'The chieftain is highly taken with you,' her uncle said abruptly.

She swung around in shock. Even though Narasimhan had made his intentions clear, she had never thought he would approach her uncle. Her uncle was the unadulterated scum of the earth and had spawned a similar offspring.

'You know, his mistresses are very well looked after. Even after he is done with him,' continued Komagan.

Mekalai could not believe her ears. Was her uncle actually suggesting that she submit to Narasimhan's advances? She knew her uncle lacked many human qualities but she was still stunned to see that he could stoop so low. Keeran continued to leer.

'You had your chance with me,' he said, baring his gold-plated teeth.

'Oh, and I am glad I missed it,' she shot back. Turning to Komagan, her eyes flashing, she asked, 'What's in it for you, Uncle? What has Narasimhan promised you in exchange for me?'

It was true, Narasimhan had commanded Komagan to bring him his niece and in exchange had promised her entire wealth to him. She wouldn't need it anyway once she was his. If her stinging retort, which was too close to the truth for comfort, didn't do it, it was her scorching, almost palpable anger that made Komagan shrink back.

Without waiting for an answer, she stormed out of the pandal. As she walked out she heard Keeran call after her, 'It's either him or me, Mekalai. You have no choice.' His malicious laughter rang loud in the air. People turned to look curiously and then whispered among themselves.

Mekalai was still shaking with anger when she reached her home. Guna was surprised to see her back so soon but knew better than to ask her why.

The next day, Arul and Lakshmi burst into her house demanding to know why she had disappeared so abruptly the previous night. Mekalai's sullen mood went unnoticed even as they chattered away about the wedding celebrations.

'What got into you? Why did you disappear like that? You missed the wedding. My god, her robes were spun from real gold and they must have weighed at least half a tonne. And she looked like she was going to faint thanks to the weight of all the jewellery,' said Arul excitedly.

'And the groom looked so handsome. I was drooling over his handlebar moustache. They say his bed has golden planks. How I wish I could find a man as rich as that,' added Lakshmi dreamily.

Hardly noticing that Mekalai remained unresponsive, the girls settled down upon the jarigai-laced straw mats, plumping the brocade and silk cushions, and plunged into an intense discussion on prospective grooms. Mekalai wandered around her room and finally settled down beside her yaazh—the harp-like instrument she was adept at playing—and began strumming absently on the gently curved bamboo bow. The girls occasionally asked her a question and she hummed an appropriate response. Guna plied them with payasam, murukku, paniyaram, and other snacks. She insisted that Mekalai eat something since she had avoided food the whole day. After much prodding, she finally nibbled on some spicy fish and rice cooked in ghee. Eventually, she caught up with the incessant chatter in time to hear the words 'highway robber' and 'messiah of the poor'. She looked up.

'What are you girls talking about?' she asked.

The girls looked at her incredulously. 'You haven't heard of the thief of Poompuhar?' asked Arul in an awed tone. 'That's all people are talking about these days. Mekalai, they say he is a phantom, not a real thing. Nobody has seen his face, no one has been able to come within miles of him,' she added, her eyes round as buttons.

'He steals from the rich and gives to the poor. Narasimhan is baying for his blood. There is a price of five thousand ingots on his head. If he is caught he will be hanged in public view,' Lakshmi further added.

With a reverential air she continued. 'But who knows if he is real. I think he is a supernatural being, a ghost of the past that haunts only the rich and the oppressive.'

'That's nonsense!' said Arul. Do you know that many young men have left the city to join his band? His strength is growing with each passing day.'

'He is said to have the strength of ten tigers,' Lakshmi whispered breathlessly.

'He can kill a boar with his bare hands...'

Even as her friends debated animatedly over this messiah's strength, appeal, and prowess not just in fighting, Mekalai's attention wandered.

She was bored. She had heard about the masked thief long before her friends had. Nithilan had told her about this messiah of the downtrodden. He had even joked that he wanted to join him. But Mekalai had found traces of truth in his jest. She sensed hero worship. She knew that he truly admired this mysterious hero who had dared to stand up against the tyrannical elite class of Poompuhar. But now Nithilan was nowhere to be found. Sometimes she wondered if he had been able to join the hero he so worshipped. As she watched twilight creep up on the town, Mekalai concluded that mysterious messiahs who didn't show themselves were of no use to her. And what was the point? He was bound to be caught and killed. Like her brother would be. The mere thought of it chilled her bones.

CHAPTER THREE

It was with a steely resolve that Mekalai decided to return to the woods and resume her practice. With Nithilan gone missing, there was no one she could turn to for help. She would now have to face Narasimhan alone. At times she wondered why he hadn't made any moves to forcibly abduct her yet. The answer lay perhaps in the fact that Narasimhan was increasingly becoming aware of his growing unpopularity. If news of his antics reached the king's ears, he could fall from grace and lose power. Maybe that was the reason why he was treading a lot more carefully than he had done in the past. But at the same time, she realized that it wouldn't last. Narasimhan was used to getting whatever he desired. And even if what he wanted proved difficult to acquire, he would stop at nothing.

Mekalai waited until midnight before she left the house. She had intentionally dressed in nondescript clothing so that even if she was spotted, no one could describe her in detail. She had chosen muslin robes of midnight blue, covered her head with a shawl and plaited her hair tightly to keep it from flying about her face during practice. She had also removed her anklets so that their jingling did not attract any attention and she could move about silently. From a distance, at best she looked like a shrouded figure.

The city was soaked in moonlight. Mekalai wound her way through the little lanes she knew so well, wanting to avoid the night guards on patrol. A girl walking about unchaperoned outside her house in the middle of the night was a taboo. What she was doing was perilous but keeping the sword in the house was even riskier. Narasimhan had put a ban on hoarding weapons at home. All weapons had to be accounted for, marked, numbered, and turned in at his military office. He probably feared a civilian uprising and was doing everything he could to prevent it.

The path to the woods at the banks of the Kaveri was deserted. She could see lights twinkling in the distance and knew that it was trading ships docking in at the harbour at the other end. A few lonely catamarans bobbed in the river, their ghostly shapes sending a shiver up her spine. She sprinted across the grassy banks into the more herbaceous border of the woods. There were a number of wells in Poompuhar, some along the river and some inside the town, and this particular one had been abandoned for years. She had discovered it when she was a child, on one of her rebellious escapades. She would dash past the guards of her home and head to the river bank to play. On one such occasion, she had wandered into the woods and discovered this well with its deep insides and iron ring steps. Hearing the guards come chasing after her, she had braved the darkness and climbed down the shaft only to find wide ledges inside, large enough for a child to hide in. Over time, the ledges had graduated from being a hiding place for dolls and trinkets to a secret vault for her precious sword. She was confident that nobody would look here. Who would climb down an old unused well in the creepy woods rumoured to be haunted by the tormented souls of people who died mysteriously under Narasimhan's reign? No one knew how these rumours had started but nobody dared to go anywhere near there, especially after sunset.

As Mekalai approached the well surrounded by a plethora of dense trees, she felt a sudden surge of excitement. The core of her being longed for adventure, and her spirit encouraged her to break the shackles of the times she lived in. These nocturnal visits to the forest symbolized freedom for her and she thrived on the excitement.

She fished out her sword and looked at it lovingly. The foliage in the woods melted deeper into the night as she practised fencing for hours, occasionally stopping to refresh herself with the cool water from the well. In the hours just before dawn, when it was darkest and when even the guards of the town had been lulled into a slumber, she decided reluctantly that it was time she went back home. She was climbing down the shaft to put the sword back when she heard the sound of a horse's hooves. A sudden fear gripped her and she stayed quietly on the little ledge inside the well, hoping it wasn't one of Narasimhan's men. Her heart was pounding and it seemed like a deafening sound in the stillness, penetrating the silence.

The sound of the hooves quietened as they approached the well. She could hear someone getting off and a horse neighing softly. She even heard him throw in the rope with the broken pitcher down into the well. The pitcher hit the water with a plop. Mekalai's pulse was racing at an awkward speed by now. What if she was found out? Who had come in the dead of the night to this abandoned well? If it was one of Narasimhan's men who had somehow followed her, then it was truly the end. She closed her eyes praying to Lord Shiva to give her strength to overcome the situation. She heard the pitcher being pulled up—the creaking pulley sounded like a tormented creature in the still of the night. She did not see anyone lean in, but instead, heard a deep voice, almost like thunder in this quiet jungle, speaking softly to the horse, urging it to drink the water. The horse neighed, almost playfully, and Mekalai heard a soft laugh. Surely none of Narasimhan's men could have such a decidedly loving timbre of voice when speaking to what was considered just an animal of convenience?

Finally Mekalai's curiosity got the better of her. She leaned over the narrow ledge in order to catch a glimpse of this unwelcome yet intriguing intruder. She realized her folly almost immediately as she tripped on a loose stone and plunged headlong into the water.

Mekalai let out a piercing scream, more out of shock than fear. She could swim like a fish but the water was stinging. And as she thrashed about in the ice-cold water in panic, she realized ruefully that she had been found out. Even if it wasn't one of Narasimhan's men, but one of the townsfolk, she was still in trouble. She would have a lot of explaining to do.

And then it happened. In a flash she felt someone land in the water next to her, someone who put out his arm and scooped her up in it. She struggled to be free and in her panic she clawed at his covered face. Maybe there was still a chance that her identity had not been discovered. It was dark inside the well, and if she could just escape his grasp, she was certain that she could use her intimate knowledge of the footholds within the well to escape from the stranger. Imagining a real possibility of escape, she struggled even harder. She could see anger in his eyes. The rest of his face was shrouded in black cloth. The two struggled in the water for some time, Mekalai silently fighting him off. But she was sure of one thing. Whoever this was he wasn't going to harm her. She somehow knew that instinctively. As the water surged around them, disturbed by the thrashing, pushing them closer, she also realized that they were uncomfortably moulded into each other. She was suddenly aware of how wet she was, how vulnerable, and how her thin robes failed to hide her voluptuous curves. She was chest deep in water and to her horror, she felt her nipples harden in response to his touch. In embarrassment coupled with confusion, Mekalai renewed her struggle and pushed herself away from him. The masked man suddenly clasped both her hands together so that she would stop flailing them around violently, and held her so close that she was unable to move.

'Stop it,' he commanded. It was a whisper, but in the silent night, it felt like a whiplash. She looked into those blazing eyes and slowly gave up her fight. As she stopped fighting him, the anger in his eyes was replaced by a certain curiosity.

Now it was two people—a man and a woman facing each other in the inky depths of a well. A man and a woman whose fates would soon get hopelessly entwined. He continued staring at this exquisite honey-hued girl with fiery eyes. Finally, after what seemed aeons, he put an arm around her waist and hoisted himself up the rope. She let him guide her out.

As she got out of the water and back to her senses, she realized that this could not be one of Narasimhan's men. Nor was he one of the townsfolk. This was indeed the masked thief of Poompuhar. And he wasn't a phantom ghost or a supernatural being. He was real, ferociously, palpably real. Real in a way that no man had ever been for her, and that knowledge itself unleashed a torrent of unidentified emotions. She knew that she was still not totally out of danger because even though he may not be anyone she knew, he could still betray her. But try as she might, she could not feel any fear or panic...just an inexplicable calm, as if she had always known they were going to meet.

They reached the top of the well and he heaved her out. He was still holding her and his rapier-sharp eyes bore into her. She was suddenly very conscious of her body. She put her hand on her chest as if to create a distance between them. She realized that she was breathing deeply and her bosom was heaving. He moved closer, his bare chest grazing her nipples. She breathed in sharply and in a flash moved away from him as though hit by a bolt of lightning. She took in his frame clothed in a black dhoti made of coarse cotton, and the distinct lack of ornamentation, save for a roughly welded iron bangle. He wore a black turban of sorts, and used its tail to cover his face effectively. His feet were bare, but she noticed a pair of leather sandals left hurriedly by the side of the well, the strong sturdy kind, worn by warriors.

Finally his deep, magnetic voice broke the silence. 'It's not impossible for a young girl to be found hiding in the well in the middle of the night, but it is unheard of. What were you doing in there?' His voice was like a cascade of gravel rolling down a mountainside, and for a second, Mekalai found herself drawn to it. She struggled against the feeling. Even though she was shaken by the unexpected turn of events, she managed to shoot him a snooty glance. 'I don't think it's any of your business,' she said haughtily. He looked at her for a while, his eyes contemplative.

'And it's a strange question coming from you, isn't it?' she added, not feeling half as brave as she managed to sound. 'You are masked, you look shady, and you too are in the woods in the middle of the night.'

He let out a chortle. 'Plucky, aren't you? Well, whatever your little secret is, it will be safe with me.' His twinkling eyes drew her in. She suddenly felt very self-conscious and vulnerable, an unusual feeling for her.

'You are the masked thief they are all talking about, aren't you?' she blurted out.

His eyes sparkled with amusement. 'Well...that depends. I may be, I may not be. After all, as you can see, I am wearing a mask, though that could just be my travel garb. And as for being a thief, have I taken anything from you without your permission?'

Mekalai felt herself blushing at the implication of what he had said. In her mind, a traitorous voice said that he probably wouldn't ever have to ask for permission to get what he wanted. He moved a little closer and she could feel his breath on her neck. 'What do you think?' he murmured huskily.

She was highly unnerved and moved back with a jolt, only to bump into the flank of his horse who neighed whimsically, as if enjoying the banter as much as his master seemed to be doing. The man's eyes, now deep pools of charcoal, with a twinkle dancing within, seemed to be assessing her. She sensed that he was further tickled by her nervousness.

'I don't think anything,' she said petulantly. 'My friends say you are not real, that you are a ghost...' Even as she said it she realized how juvenile she sounded. And when he threw back his head and laughed, she regretted it immediately.

He took her hand and chuckled. 'Would you like to pinch me to see if I am real?' She shot him a dirty look but said nothing.

'Or maybe there are other ways in which I could prove to you I am real,' he said in a low voice. The inflection in his voice was unmistakable.

She could hardly believe what she was hearing and she turned away, her wet shiny hair grazing his chest as she did. She could feel his breath on her bare back and somewhere from the recesses of her being, desire stirred within her. She was aghast that this masked intruder, this impudent thug could make her feel that way. She felt him leaning towards her, taking in a deep breath, and reaching around her. Trapped between the horse and the well-toned body of her rescuer, Mekalai felt like she was losing control of herself.

'What...what do you think you're doing?' she heard herself say, hating the huskiness that crept in involuntarily into her voice. The movement of the man stilled behind her, and from the corner of her eye, she saw him pull a blanket off the horse's saddle. Turning her around, he wrapped the blanket around her. 'Just making sure that the cold night doesn't reach your bones.' His eyes danced with mischief. 'What did you think?'

Stung by the transparency of her own emotions, Mekalai pushed away from the man, dropping the blanket on the ground. 'I'm going home,' she said firmly, and started to walk away. He watched her for a few seconds.

'Narasimhan's men are prowling on the river bank,' he said quietly.

She stopped right there. But she didn't look back. He untied his horse and came close to her.

'Get on the horse,' he said commandingly, all traces of humour gone. It was a voice she wanted to trust. She obeyed him without a word, though still maintaining her haughty stance. They rode silently. She was aware of his strong arms that reached around her in order to hold the reins of the horse. They rode on through the dark lanes. He seemed to know his way around. The moon too had disappeared, leaving the town in darkness. She directed him towards her house and when they came to her lane, he set her down.

'You'll have to go on your own from here. I shouldn't come further,' he said. Before she could even respond to what he'd said, he turned his stallion and rode away into the murky depths of the night. She didn't know how long she stood there watching him disappear before she managed to find her way back to her house in a trance-like state. What had just happened seemed like a dream to her.

That night sleep eluded Mekalai for a very long time. And when it finally came, it brought with it hazy dreams of a masked man on a horse with deep, dark, beautiful eyes. When she woke up the next morning, Mekalai wondered if it had all been a dream, a thrilling, romantic, and slightly erotic dream. She had had an encounter with the masked thief of Poompuhar, a feat no one could really boast of. Colour rose to her cheeks even as she remembered the vivid details of their encounter last night. She remembered how her body had, for the first time, reacted to a man's touch. She cringed with embarrassment as she recalled how her nipples had suddenly come alive when they came into contact with him. His rippling muscles, his wide, smooth chest, his bronzed, suntanned skin flashed through her memory and she felt her cheeks burn scarlet. She closed her eyes and imagined his lips on hers. Flushed, she opened her eyes in a flash and smacked herself on the head. Sensible girls from good families did not fall in love with strange, mysterious thugs. They obeyed social conventions and married respectable traders, merchants, officers, or soldiers. And surely, this could not be love. It seemed more like desire, lust to her. She had heard her friends talk unendingly of their feelings about different men, so maybe this was what it was. But surely what she had felt right now could not be so trivial as normal flirtation.

This was the first time a man had had such an effect on her. She had never felt even the slightest flutter of attraction for anyone before. She wondered if she should feel deep shame at her feelings and decided that she need not. It was nobody's business but hers. And whom was she going to tell anyway?

When Guna entered Mekalai's chamber carrying her morning milk and fruit, she noticed that her mistress seemed unduly listless. She kept staring into space and didn't even take notice when Guna placed the tray next to her. The girl was perplexed but knew better than to disturb her temperamental mistress.

After her bath and morning puja, Mekalai decided to pay her friend Arul a visit. Perhaps her incessant chatter would drown out the thoughts of the mysterious stranger that seemed to have gripped her. Sitting at home would only make her more restless and she wanted to get the events of the previous night out of her mind. Today, she picked out a simple yellow cotton robe with the colourful, hand-painted design on the border that was the rage at the time. Due to her dislike for earrings, she left her ears defiantly bare but slipped on her nose ring and her toe rings. She especially liked the one she had put on today with a stud shaped like a fish. Silver anklets tinkled on her feet as she sprinted out of the house.

Arul lived three lanes away, in a mansion almost as large as Mekalai's. Unlike Mekalai though, Arul had a large family. In addition to her parents, Arul had six younger siblings, one unmarried aunt, who lived with them, and a widowed maternal uncle who liked to pinch unsuspecting maids' bottoms. He never went further but this one oddity had earned him the tag of a womanizer. But at the helm was Avai Paati, the dowager grandmother who still ruled the household with an iron hand. She was at least eighty years old, knew every dash of gossip worth knowing, was steeped in tales of yore, and adored Mekalai. She loved the girl's spirit even if she made a show of disapproval and worried for her now that her only brother had gone missing. Seated on her plush velvet and silk couch, her five remaining teeth stained with paan, a generous moustache, and her eyes smeared with kohl, she looked a bit like a large, though slightly shrivelled walrus dressed in Kanchipuram silk.

'Ah, my girl,' she chirped, seeing Mekalai, her shield-like nose stud gleaming as it caught the sunlight. Mekalai smiled and sat down beside her.

'You have left your hair loose again. How old do you think you are?' Avai Paati admonished, and immediately proceeded to plait Mekalai's knee-length hair. She made the knots impossibly tight and Mekalai winced.

'Serves you right,' said Avai Paati severely. 'Walking around with loose hair and attracting all the wrong attention.'

'I am bound to attract all the wrong attention even if I were bald,' said Mekalai sullenly. 'I seem to have a gift.'

Avai eyed her sharply. She knew all about Narasimhan and his immoral advances. Her experience told her that things would soon come to a head and Mekalai would have to literally choose between the devil and the deep sea. If she valued her honour, that is. 'Why don't you go away for some time,' she suggested gently. 'Go to my sister's in Madurai. You can lie low for a while and when things cool down, you can return.'

Mekalai shook her head. 'No, I must be here in

case Nithilan returns.' She thought she saw a flash of pity in the old woman's eyes. She realized that everyone thought her brother to be dead. They were sure that Narasimhan's men had caught and killed him and buried him deep in the woods. But her heart did not agree; it told her that he was still alive.

'Tell me about Narasimhan, Paati,' she said suddenly. 'Was he always this evil?'

'Yes, my child. Unfortunately, evil takes a human shape very often,' said Avai shaking her head. 'Narasimhan's father Kumaraselvan was a noble man. But his first wife, Narasimhan's mother, was the worst thing that could have happened to him. She was shrewish, diabolic, and cruel—traits that she passed on to her son. Kumaraselvan married again, a poor girl with whom he had genuinely fallen in love, and she bore him a son. A good boy who was a lot like his father. Kumaraselvan realized that his older son was unworthy to be his heir and instead decided that his younger one should inherit his name and wealth.' The old lady let out a deep sigh. 'Mekalai, here is proof that real evil exists in this world. Narasimhan murdered his old father in his bed one night and kidnapped the poor second wife and her son. They were never heard of again. Some say he has kept them alive in the dungeons of his fortress, others say they were murdered and their bodies thrown into the sea. It is also said that the young boy who must have been just nine or ten years old at that time, put up a real fight before he went down.' Tears glistened in Avai's eyes as she relived one of the saddest and most appalling stories of her times.

Mekalai listened in horror. She felt sick to her stomach. Tears stung her eyes as she thought of the little boy who had lost his life for no fault of his. Or had he? Was he still alive, wasting away in a dank dungeon without even the slightest trace of sunlight? If he had been alive, he would have been just a few years older than Nithilan, she reflected. Her horror slowly turned to rage. No one should ever be allowed to get away with something like this. Was there no justice in this world? Avai's words jerked her out of her reverie. The old lady said, 'Manikottai transformed from a happy home into a horrendous structure bathed in blood and malevolence.'

Arul's mother entered, reminding the old lady that it was time for her afternoon nap. 'She gets cranky otherwise and we have to bear the brunt,' she explained to Mekalai. As Mekalai helped the old woman on to her feet it struck her to ask one more thing. 'Paati,' she said, almost coyly. 'What do you think of the masked thief?'

Avai Paati chuckled. It made her triple chin quiver. 'Ah...I think he sounds wonderful. We all need a messiah. Now if only he really existed.'

'What if he did exist?' Mekalai asked curiously.

'I would ask him to come and sweep you off your feet,' the old lady replied laughingly. 'I have a feeling he could keep a woman happy,' she cackled. With that she shuffled out of the room, leaning on her golden walking stick and leaving Mekalai blushing.

Mekalai watched her leave and then spoke under her breath, 'He does exist Paati, he does...'

She spent the rest of the afternoon playing palaankuzhi with Arul's younger sisters on the terrace until their brothers interrupted by pelting them with mango kernels. Pandemonium ensued after that and when Mekalai left the house, the children were still yelling at the top of their voices and kernels were still flying around. Her heart felt considerably lighter as she walked back to her own house. The stately gates flanked by traditional terracotta horses swung open to let her in. The mansion, an impressive structure of brick and mortar, gleamed opulently in the sun. Intricate paintings of gods and goddesses adorned the walls and the pools shimmered with exotic lotus and lilies.

When she entered her expansive, sunlit drawing room, she found Guna in a state of unfettered excitement. Guna ran to her mistress, holding out a rough parchment. 'It came in through the window,' she announced in high-pitched frenzy. 'It has Master's seal on it.'

Mekalai grabbed the parchment from her and read it, her hands shaking. The letter was brief but reassuring.

Dearest sister,

I hope this letter finds you well and happy. I am extremely sorry for not establishing contact before but it was just too dangerous. I want you to know that I am safe. And I will come back very soon. In the meantime, please know that even if I am not with you, no harm can come to you. I assure you of that. I cannot say any more at this point.

Yours lovingly,

Nithilan.

Her tears fell on the parchment and when she finally looked up to see Guna's distressed face she let out a small laugh. 'Silly girl, these are tears of joy. My brother is alive.'

Guna's face broke into a smile too and she clapped her hands loudly. Mekalai sprinted up the dark wooden staircase with its ornate brass railing, to her chamber. She flung herself on her bed, still sobbing with happiness. Then the questions began to arise in her mind. Where had he written from? Who was he with? Her deeper instincts told her he was hiding in the woods, the same woods she frequented every other night, the same woods where she had encountered the notorious masked thief. It did not take Mekalai long to put two and two together. Her brother must have definitely joined his hero. There was no doubt. And somehow, that knowledge came as a relief to her. She had a sudden temptation to ride out into the woods and find him but she quickly put the thought to rest. It was much too dangerous. There was a good chance that she was being closely watched and even though she was willing to risk her own life by venturing out at night, she didn't want to place her brother's life in any further danger. Or the masked man's, she suddenly realized. She didn't want anything to happen to him either. She was instantly cross with herself for thinking of him. It also occurred to her that he had been on her mind ever since their nocturnal tryst in the forest. Mekalai felt confused and wondered why this was happening to her. And why was she behaving like a lovesick puppy? Did she have any dearth of male attention? She could have any man she wanted. The thought did nothing to cheer her up, so she went to her music room and strummed on her yaazh, praying for the cloud over her mind to lift.

CHAPTER FOUR

THE WOODS THAT MEKALAI so frequently visited stood on the banks of the river Kaveri just before it united with the sea. It was generally considered unlucky to go into them and over time, many myths and legends had been spun around them, most distinctly macabre, which succeeded in keeping the people away from them. Grandmothers told their grandchildren scary bedtime stories of ogres and demons who inhabited the woods; and of headless soldiers who roamed around the edges looking for replacement heads. They spoke of flesh-eating female vampires who could be recognized by the fact that their feet never touched the ground. They were mostly found hanging from drumstick trees and when they saw a potential victim arrive, they would assume the most inviting human form to lure them. These stories and myths served their purpose and no man or woman ever wished to set foot inside the woods. Except, of course, Mekalai.

Even as a child, Mekalai had thrived on flouting the common rules of behaviour, much to her mother's chagrin. As she grew older, despite the changes in her life and the loss of her parents, that rebellious aspect of her personality had not changed. Even as the tales of the famed devils who lived in these forests started taking hold of the collective imagination of the townsfolk, Mekalai couldn't help but be drawn to seeing for herself what this hell looked like. The first time she had gone into those woods had been by chance. Having gotten used to spending hours by herself, Mekalai wandered into the forests looking for wild berries. The deeper she went, the more fascinated she was by the gentle quiet breeze that whistled through the leaves and played with her hair. Once or twice, she was certain that she had glimpsed a passing shadow, but then the light had changed and she had seen the forest for what it was—a safe haven away from prying eyes. Mekalai had returned thereafter, often many times a day, and soon it had turned into an oasis of calm amidst the chaos around her. Her frequent visits had reinforced her belief that nothing supernatural or horrifying lived there. Except...sometimes she was sure that she wasn't the only one there.

It was on the strength of these legends that a tall, lean man with coal-black eyes had established his secret stronghold in the forest. He had made it his home, his territory where no one dared to trespass. It suited him fine that even the bravest of men didn't dare to go beyond the fringes of the forest. It was here, in the unfathomable depths of the forest, that he had built his life and the myths surrounding it.

Sometimes, while walking through the woods, he too had felt an unseen presence around him...something that told him that perhaps there were others as well for whom the foliage provided a haven. But he had never yet chanced upon anyone. This was fortunate, because had any stranger met this well-built warrior, and known the reward that had been put on his head, he would have been tempted to try and capture him. This would be unfortunate for the hapless stranger, because his attempt would only have led to a battle with a foregone conclusion. For the warrior was none other than the masked thief of Poompuhar, a man so used to being hunted, and so skilled in the art of battle and cunning, that any person who chose to take him on would only have learnt a lesson in humility. The masked thief of Poompuhar...the name amused him. It had a distinct, notorious ring to it. What amused him more was the fact that Narasimhan's military men, irritated by the fact that they had never even seen him, had fabricated such fantastic stories about him. And the gullible townspeople were inclined to believe them.

He himself had in fact been instrumental in making the soldiers spread the stories that they anyway believed to be true. He smiled at the memory. One evening, the soldiers were guarding a convoy of jewels through these woods, worried that the dreaded thief would attack them and steal their booty. At the sight of a solitary horse tied to one of the many sapling trees of the forest, they fanned out, setting a trap.

The thief realized that the only way out was either a bloodbath or...maybe just plain humour. Creeping laterally through the forest, always keeping the enemy in sight, he started throwing pebbles in the direction of the soldiers, now separated in smaller groups. Having attracted their attention, he started screaming, as if in pain. The soldiers gingerly approached the man who lay writhing on the mossy floor of the forest.

'What is the matter?' the soldier at the forefront asked with trepidation. The thief continued to scream. Finally, when everyone had gathered around him, he stopped dramatically, pointed at the leader with a flourish and sighed, 'Tomorrow...tomorrow.' Then he collapsed on the floor. The soldiers, not realizing that this was the very robber they had come to arrest, looked confusedly at their leader. The thief, satisfied with the impact he had made, then sat up, as if awoken from a trance and said, 'The yakshi...the vampire goddess...she...she...took possession of me.' Everyone was shocked. By this time, the leader of the search party, his face drained of all colour, ordered his battalion to move out of the forest. As they left, the trap forgotten, the thief was certain he heard the sergeant muttering 'Tomorrow...what about tomorrow?'

From that day on, ten years ago, the rumours had started spreading like wildfire. Every time merchandise carts were stopped and looted, and coffers emptied, the rumours grew stronger. He also reflected that people were inclined to believe in violence more than anything else. It was an accepted norm that thugs, thieves, and pirates were violent, inflicting harm on their victims. But the masked thief of Poompuhar was not violent. He did not torture his victims or chop off their heads. He did not tie them to stakes and leave them to burn and die. He merely lightened their purses and their treasure chests. Hence, he could not be human.

This young man, who knew the woods, also knew every nook and cranny of Poompuhar. He knew where the diamond merchant, whose palatial abode stood outside the temple, kept all his ill-gotten wealth. He knew where the rich, unwed middle-aged heiress who was fond of betting, kept her gold ingots, so that she could find them readily. He was aware of the black market for smuggled gems, horses, and ivory. He knew the meeting point for the Roman traders to sell their wares to the local merchants in return for illegal goods. This was so because despite the fact that no one claimed to have ever met him or seen him, over the years, he had built a fantastic band of followers and spies. These were like-minded young men who had tired of their wealthy fathers and their unending greed and oppression. These were youngsters who had been wronged by Narasimhan and his vile ways. These were men who were determined to win justice even if it was by unconventional methods.

They followed their leader without ever questioning him, and if an aspirant wanted to join their clan they found him before he could find them. It was not a large band but it was determined and close-knit.

Only this handful of men knew the masked thief's name. Most were unaware of his past. They didn't know who he really was, what his parentage was, or any of the circumstances leading up to him becoming this feared entity. All they knew was that they could trust him and count on him. As he gave his beloved black stallion a rubdown with mustard oil, the image of a drenched, dangerously beautiful damsel flashed in his head. His hands stilled of their own volition as his mind travelled back to the previous night. He remembered the fire in her eyes, the sullen fullness of her mouth. He recalled how fragrant she had smelt when he had leaned close to her. He had almost reached for her soft skin... The thief pulled back from the memory as if stung by a bee. The horse, as if sensing his master's disorientation, let out a soft whinny of sympathy. Brought back to reality, the man smiled at himself, amused by his own reaction. From the time he was a boy, he had known that women found him intriguing. At over six feet, and lithe with an athletic gait, he was hard to miss. But while he was definitely good-looking, what really made the women quiver with delight was his charm and his tremendous skill with the paintbrush. Invariably, whenever he walked through the town, carrying his chalks and his brushes, he would be invited into a household with a request for a painting. But he had always known that that wasn't all they hoped to get from him. The women crowded around him, trying to attract him with their unwavering attention and seductive ways. And what infuriated them was that he was never interested. Even when he grew older, and indulged himself in the ways of the world, he had never known anyone who had stayed in his mind longer than a few nights.

But last night was different... He couldn't forget her petulance, her resolve, her courage. She had held a volatile secret close to her heart that she had not revealed to him. And he could not mistake the turbulence in her spirit and in her eyes. And that body...It wasn't as though he had no experience with women but this girl had had an effect on him that he couldn't control. He wished he could see her again, feel her soft skin against his, and look into her ocean-deep eyes. He was jolted out of his reverie when his horse neighed indignantly as if finally tired of being ignored.

'Were you thinking about her too?' he asked the horse. The horse neighed in response.

'Vikraman!' a voice called out. A stocky young man came running to him.

'Yes, Nithilan,' said Vikraman—the thief, the cunning prankster, and the painter.

'I have some good news and some bad news,' Nithilan said. Bemused, Vikraman gestured to him to continue. 'The good news is that a bullfight is soon going to be held at the town square. The merchants' association has organized it.'

Vikraman's eyes gleamed. Manji virattu or bullfighting was a sport he had always enjoyed. He lived for the thrill of fighting a raging bull, looking into the mad whites of its eyes, till it tamed under his powerful force.

Nithilan looked at his leader's face. 'Now for the bad news.' Vikraman already knew what was coming but he let Nithilan speak. 'Vikraman, I know you love this dangerous sport but greater danger lies ahead for you if you go into the town. It is fine when you go to the smaller villages to take part in bullfighting, but this is Poompuhar...outside of this forest, the soldiers are always on the lookout. They are waiting for us...'

'Makes it all the more tempting, doesn't it?' said Vikraman, his eyes shining with excitement. 'Besides, who knows what I look like? Who knows that the masked thief and I are one?'

Nithilan hesitated. If Vikraman were to go, then so could he. Maybe Mekalai would be there and he could catch a glimpse of her, even talk to her. But he would have to be heavily disguised. All of Poompuhar knew him. They would recognize him in an instant. As if to mirror his thoughts, Vikraman said, 'I would like you to come with me if I do decide to participate. I know you are longing to meet your sister. Do you know if she is safe?'

Nithilan frowned. No, he didn't. He had managed to send her a message through one of the men who had gone into town to collect provisions, but he had no way of getting an answer. He was quite certain that Narasimhan wouldn't go after her in an outright manner now that his reputation was at stake, but there was no saying what tricks he would try. He wanted to make sure his sister was fine.

Vikraman put a comforting hand on his aide's shoulder and said, 'Don't worry, she will be safe.' He moved away to put a huge skinned boar on the sooty spit on the ground. Rubbing the meat with salt and pepper, he added, 'Soon all this will be over and Poompuhar will become the heaven it once used to be.' There was a determined glint in his eye as he said this. And Nithilan knew what he meant and hoped with all his heart that it would come true.

That evening Vikraman decided that he would go into town and pretend to be a young painter in search of work. Indira Vizha, the festival in honour of Lord Indra, that was so widely celebrated in all of Tamilakkam was round the corner and the town would be in need of decorators and painters. It lasted for about twenty eight days and each day was spent in glorious celebrations. The town was spruced up, cleaned, and decorated. The boom of drums could be heard throughout the day; yajnas were conducted and musical performances were held amidst great pomp and fanfare.

Vikraman decided to head straight to the Murugan temple, the shrine that was usually the fulcrum of the town's activity. It was another power centre in the town, employing the largest number of people. He knew he could blend in easily there. These occasional visits to the town as an amiable, earnest painter in search of work also gave him access to the information he needed. People generally talked around those who didn't unnerve them and Vikraman didn't unnerve them in the least. He mostly came across as the 'friendly boy looking for work'.

He slipped into modest robes of white, wrapped a thin cloth around his upper arm where there was a long, thin scar, and draped a piece of old silk around his head. He rode on his stallion till the edge of the woods along with a member of his tribe and then sent the stallion back with him. He walked along the grassy banks of the river, enjoying the moist breeze that blew his way. As he entered the town he knew so well, he felt a surge of emotion. He wound his way through the shady lanes down to the temple grounds. The temple was a huge brick-and-plaster structure dedicated to Lord Murugan. There were three other temples in the vicinity, dedicated to Shiva, Parvathi, and Ganapathi. The temple square was lined with women selling little thaalis of flowers, kumkum, and incense sticks to offer to the Lord. Other women sat selling little terracotta dolls, bangles, and other trinkets. Minstrels wandered around, singing hymns in their sonorous voices. Elephants stood outside the temple, swaying pompously, their trunks decorated with vermilion and sandalwood. Vikraman bought a bunch of bananas from one of the vendors and fed the elephants. Then he found an empty corner and sat down. He took out a little bundle of coloured chalks and began to draw on the ground. He drew Murugan on the peacock in vivid colours, and passers-by halted curiously to take a look at his striking handiwork. Soon enough, just as he expected, one of the temple officials came running out telling him to get out as this was temple property. Vikraman apologized and then proceeded to show off his work to the harrowed official. He said he was in urgent need of work. After some minutes of intense persuasion, Vikraman managed to land himself a job as a mural painter for the walls of the Parvathi temple. He packed up his chalk pieces and headed in that direction.

Later that evening, he went in search of Nithilan's house. He followed the directions he had been given and realized that he was in the same lane where he had dropped off the girl the other night. His heart was pounding as he walked down the flower-dotted road trying to find the mansion with the blue windows. It couldn't be missed. And then he saw her. She was standing at the blue window and almost instinctively, his breath quickened.

Mekalai stood framed at the topmost window of her house, the evening sun shimmering in her hair. She must have just bathed, Vikraman thought to himself, as he took in her wet hair, her naked shoulders and the thin cloth with which she had wrapped herself while she waited for her clothes to be laid out. But most importantly, he saw her staring out unseeingly in the direction of the forest, a slight smile on her lips. Was she thinking of him, of that night? Could she really be somehow happy at the memory? Even as

Vikraman let out a sigh, a shadow crossed her face and her smile faded. Vikraman couldn't stop staring at the vision.

She did not notice the man standing on the opposite side of the lane, looking up at her. Vikraman continued to stare as if he had seen an angel. And an angel she was. For a moment, he forgot that this was Nithilan's younger sister. He took in her smooth, creamy skin, her large, slanting eyes, her graceful neck, and her full figure. In that instant he knew he wanted her, he wanted to run his fingers through her raven hair, he wanted to place his lips on her rosebud mouth... Just then, Mekalai felt his eyes on her and she looked down, to see this utterly striking man looking up at her. To her horror, she blushed; and quickly shrank back from the window.

Vikraman willed her to return to the window, wondering what she had seen in him that would make the feisty vixen of that night step into the shadows like a touch-me-not. He waited for a while, but soon it became clear that the young woman who had been on his mind almost constantly was not going to return. Disappointed, Vikraman returned to the temple grounds.

From the other side of the windows, Mekalai watched his retreating back and wondered what had come over her. A strange man stared at her and she blushed like a simpering village belle? Something stirred inside her...even though she had not seen him closely, he seemed vaguely familiar. She could not find an answer. Surely, it was a definite improvement from being stared at by lecherous middle-aged merchants, she reflected with a wry smile.

A folk play was to be staged at the mandapam of the Parvathi temple and the town was buzzing with activity. When Arul and Lakshmi came to fetch her to watch the play, Mekalai was ready. She had chosen robes of flaming orange and deep green. Her hands tinkled with the lac bangles interspersed with gold and diamond bracelets that she had bought recently. Guna had insisted on plaiting her hair today and little diamond pins adorned each knot. Encouraged by getting her way, Guna had also insisted on jasmine gajras. Mekalai slipped on her favourite hamsa besari nose stud, which was intricately shaped like a swan, studded with miniature diamonds. As she surveyed herself in the mirror before leaving, she was pleased with the results.

Arul's father had insisted that the girls be chaperoned by her aunt and that they should go in the chariot. So the girls bundled into the huge chariot along with Arul's garrulous aunt and sped away to the temple hall, which was situated right outside the temple grounds. All through the ride, the aunt kept sighing and reliving the glory of her youth. 'When I was young,' she began and Arul rolled her eyes. 'When I was young, I had no dearth of suitors. Why, the king's chief accountant was besotted with me. Alas, he was already married with five children. My father would not hear of it.' She sighed sadly.

They had gotten through seven other prospective matches that were not meant to be by the time they finally arrived at the temple. As she alighted from the chariot, her pudgy feet making a splotch on the ground, the aunt had one last pearl of wisdom to impart. She caught hold of Mekalai's arm and said, 'See these breasts?' she said indicating her massive bosom which resembled a large, squishy watermelon. 'They used to be the envy of Poompuhar once. They were magnificent in their youth. Women envied me, men wanted me. Now they look like sacks of dried grapes. Find a man soon, or your youth too will wane and then the men won't care whether you exist or not.'

Mekalai muttered something unintelligible, not really knowing what to say, while her friends stifled their giggles. As they trooped in, the aunt issued further instructions. 'If you do not lock eyes with every simpleton in sight, it would help. Look demure and coy. Reserve your flirtations for the eligible ones.'

Arul of course wasted no time making eyes at a young flute player at the other end of the hall. The bright-eyed youth played along, flattered by the attention. Thankfully, the play was just about to begin as they entered the mandapam. Mekalai looked around, trying to find seats towards the front. The mandapam was richly decorated with flowers and lamps. The stage, which was just a portion of the mandapam, was marked by colourful rugs on the floor. The lights were shadowy yet not dim, and the mood was distinctly celebratory. The actors took centre stage. It was a scene out of the battle of Kurukshetra from the *Mahabharata*. The actors sang in clear tones and Mekalai was soon lost in the play. The colours were kaleidoscopic and the drama ran high. An hour later, when the play ended, it was announced that after a short interval some singers from Thanjavur would present a recital to wind up the evening. Mekalai looked around. Arul and Lakshmi seemed deep in animated conversation with the lead actor of the play, a swarthy, broad-chested youth who had played Arjuna. The flute player had long been discarded in favour of the actor. She could hear them giggling uncontrollably and the actor puffed out his chest more and more with each passing minute. She had no interest in joining them and instead decided to walk around to the back of the temple where drinking water was available.

The path was dark and there was hardly anybody there. Mekalai's steps rang out in the dark. She found the cool stone fountain and gulped down water. Refreshed, she turned her steps back towards the mandapam and collided with someone in the dark. He caught her fall, putting an arm around her waist and when she looked up, she found it was the man who had been staring at her that afternoon from below her window. Their faces came close and she could feel his hot breath on her eyes. In a single audacious moment, he bent a little lower and lightly grazed her lips with his. The shock of it shot through her like a sharp bolt of lightning. Time stopped and her senses blurred except for the painful sliver of desire that raced through her body. Without meaning to, without thinking, she responded. This time it was a real kiss, not just a hazy impact. He kissed her with a newfound confidence and expertise. She could taste his salty lips, and feel his urgency. He gently nipped her lower lip and she let out a little moan. She felt the world spin around her and wildly clutched his shoulder.

'I want you,' he said huskily. He pulled her closer and she didn't resist. His mouth was still hot on hers... Mekalai closed her eyes. In the distance, fireworks exploded and the noise brought both of them back to their senses. Mekalai sprang back and he let her go. 'I am not sure what just happened here,' she said, her eyes flashing, her breath coming in gasps.

'Wait, let me think,' the stranger drawled lazily. 'I kissed you and you kissed me back.'

'How dare you...' she shot back, her voice shaking.

He raised his eyebrows. 'How dare I? Lady, I must remind you that when I kissed you, you didn't pull back. In fact, I distinctly remember you responding.'

Mekalai winced at the memory. He was right. Utter disbelief at what she had just done washed over her. Now she couldn't even face this impudent man, she could barely look him in the eye. And something about him seemed so familiar. She knew she had never met him before and yet she got a feeling of déjà vu. Assailed by all these thoughts and disturbed by the young man who continued to stand there with an amused grin on his rakishly handsome face, she turned and ran. She ran as fast as she could till she reached the mandapam. Arul and Lakshmi were waiting there impatiently for her.

'Mekalai! Where do you keep disappearing to? And what happened? Why is your hair all undone?' asked Arul impatiently.

Mekalai hurriedly smoothed her hair and said, 'I went to get a drink of water. Where's your aunt?'

'She has spotted a prospective match for herself,' said Arul, looking totally exasperated. 'He is a pearl merchant from Madurai, with a face like a wizened monkey. And he looks at least two hundred years old and is missing most of his teeth. But then, my aunt isn't exactly an apsara so it's a match made in heaven.'

'Let's leave quickly before she discovers he has sons who have been blessed with their father's good looks and charm and she decides to matchmake,' giggled Lakshmi and they made their way to the entrance where the chariot was waiting. Later when she looked back on the events of the day, Mekalai had no memory of the ride back home. It was a complete blur. Her friends took no notice of her silence and chatted away while Mekalai remained in a state of trance-like numbness.

As soon as she reached home, she threw off her adornments in a state of frenzy. Guna came running wondering what the matter was but Mekalai shut the door in her face. She fell on her bed, her hair flowing like a river and she closed her eyes. She could still feel the taste of his lips, his touch on her body... She couldn't imagine what had come over her. How could she kiss a total stranger? What had brought on such wanton behaviour? And why did he seem so familiar? Where had she seen him before? And to top it all, she still felt attracted to the masked thief. 'You run the risk of turning into a slut, Mekalai,' she told herself severely. Maybe she should start tying up her hair instead of leaving it open, and hence attracting all this unwelcome attention, she thought. She chose not to address the shocking desire she felt for two men—total strangers—and the knowledge that her reaction had nothing to do with how her hair was done.

Her eyes finally closed in exhaustion, well past midnight. Her last thought was that she wanted to see him again. In her sleep-addled state, she couldn't figure out who it was that she wanted to see again—the masked thief or the stranger at the temple. Images flickered in front of her half-closed eyes but before she could fight them, she fell into a deep dreamless slumber.

She felt no better the next morning. She lightly fingered her lip where he had gently nipped it and she felt a tinge of the passion she had experienced the night before. She sat there in her cool, airy chamber until past noon, and then decided to go for a walk to shake herself out of her indolent state.

At the other end of the town, Vikraman was crouched by the farthest end of the temple walls, painting murals. He was unable to stop thinking about Mekalai. Even as his hands absently traced near-perfect lines on the plastered surface, fragments of last night floated in his mind. He too had lain awake for ages thinking about the girl who had taken over his heart, mind, and life. There was fire there and there was ice. She was unpredictable, like a sudden change of season. But he realized he had to control himself. There was no future that he could foresee with Mekalai. His life was steeped in peril and he could hardly draw a woman into it. Moreover, she was Nithilan's sister. He couldn't imagine any brother wanting his sister to be with a man whose future seemed poised at the edge of a precipice. The thought dampened his mood and he continued painting. Around sundown, he decided to pack up for the day and head back to the lodgings he had taken up near the riverside. As he walked back, the golden sun framing his graceful figure, he made up his mind that as soon as the bull fight was over, he would return to the woods and try his best to keep out of her way forever. But a little voice in his head seemed to just laugh cruelly and disbelievingly at the idea...

Mekalai sat by the river bank, watching the glowing sun dip into the sea. Just as the last, perfectly rimmed bit disappeared fierily into the water, she got up to go back home. To her utter horror, she saw a figure approach from a distance. Even from the outline she could tell who it was. No no no, now was not the time to bump into that impudent rake again. She quickened her pace, wanting to disappear round the corner before he could spot her; but a herder with his cows was coming her way. The creatures lumbered on at their own pace, arresting hers and she was forced to stop and let them pass. She could hear distinct footsteps behind her and she closed her eyes tightly as if that would make her invisible. If only life was that simple.

Vikraman couldn't believe his eyes. It was a like a sign from above. Just when he had made up his mind never to set his eyes on Mekalai again, here she was in electrifying flesh and blood. It was like looking into a dazzling light—that was the effect of her blinding beauty. All his notions of never seeing her again disappeared, and in that moment, he knew he had to have her. Now and forever. He saw her waiting to let the cows pass, her body quivering and he instantly knew she had seen him too.

As he drew close, he could feel his heart pounding thunderously. She turned to face him. He felt the hair on his arms rise. 'If I may ask, why are you following me around?' she asked haughtily. 'I will set the town guards on you for such impudence.'

Vikraman threw back his head and laughed. 'It is not I who is following you, but you who has been haunting me.' The words had their desired effect. Uncertainty flickered in her eyes.

She said in a low voice, 'Listen, about what happened yesterday...I am not really like that...I don't...I don't...'

'Go around kissing strange men?' he finished for her, his mouth twisted into a teasing smile.

'Yes,' she spat. 'It was a huge mistake and I can assure you it will never happen again.'

'And I can assure you it will,' he said in a velveteen tone, coming closer.

She took a step back as her turbulent eyes bore into his. And then another one. Finally she turned and like a light-footed deer, scurried away.

He stood there, watching her go. She didn't turn back once. As she faded from sight, he realized with a pang that this was a point of no return for him. They were bound together inexplicably. She was his destiny and he was hers and he would do everything he had to do to make things right and have her in his life.

That night, while the stars twinkled, someone with exquisite feline grace jumped over the walls of Mekalai's mansion. That someone was so quiet that the doddering guard at the gate didn't even hear a stone turn. There was a gleam in his eyes as he entered the grounds. Fate be damned. He was going to gamble dangerously with it. And win....

CHAPTER FIVE

MEKALAI HAD RETURNED HOME in a state of heightened fury mixed with a numbness. She had been restless, pacing the room, not comfortable in any place she chose to rest. She barely sat down to do one thing when she would give it up and look to do another. As the night deepened, Mekalai threw away the piece of gay embroidery she had been attempting all evening listlessly—the design unintelligible to her in her current state of mental and emotional disarray. Finally, lying down on her bed, she was forced to come to terms with herself. She knew that the reason for her sleeplessness and fury was that she was angry for being so attracted to this stranger. She didn't even know his name. And she had kissed him. And touched him. And let him touch her. She also knew in her heart that there had been something so erotic in the way that the stranger had presumed to kiss her...as if she, Mekalai, only daughter of a wealthy merchant, was nothing but a woman whose role was to pleasure him. Nobody in the world would dare, but he had...and what was worse, she had let him. His audacity intrigued her. Somehow, in the shifting shadows of the night, that kiss had seemed the most solid, the most real thing in her world. She hated that she couldn't hate him, that she couldn't regret the moment, much as she wanted to, much as she knew she would feel better if she did. And why was she dwelling on it so much? And why did he bother her the way he did? Mekalai sat up in her bed again, a new thought in her head. He was just another womanizing cad who thought he could take what he wanted as he pleased. Only, she reluctantly conceded, she hadn't really minded, had she? It wasn't as if he had forcibly kissed her or molested her. She had responded, wanting it as much as he had. And this bothered her more than anything else. She fell back on the bed, covering her face with a silken sheet, but her thoughts could not be silenced. Of course he was good-looking. Even in his simple garments, his bearing had an unmistakable stamp of aristocracy. With his aquiline nose, his strong jaw with the cleft in his chin, the straight eyebrows that arched over twinkling brown eyes, even the small mark just below his eye, almost like a sparing scar, he hardly seemed one of the peasantfolk. Despite herself, her thoughts ran to his body—the comforting breadth of his shoulders, his narrow waist, and his strong chest. She thought of his deep, unfathomable eyes and how they had glazed over with lust, and his determined mouth that had pressed down upon hers so confidently. He had a raw, sensuous power and she had been drawn to it like a moth to a flame.

She threw off her bedcover restlessly and tossed and turned. The night seemed to linger on endlessly. She desperately wanted sleep to take over, so that she could wake up the next morning and discover that all this had been one long strange dream. Her father always used to say that the new morning brought with it new memories. Maybe tomorrow she would remember something different, anything else but the look in the man's eyes as he pulled her closer, breathing in her fragrance before letting his lips touch hers. Mekalai sighed at that forgotten little detail that had clearly ingrained itself into her subconscious as her body had responded to his touch. Mekalai looked out of the window, wondering when some blessed sleep would come her way and pull her out of her tortuous restlessness. But it was only when the inky hue of the sky had started fading that sleep touched her eyelids.

Dawn crept over Poompuhar and the town lit up in a golden glow. A koel sang its chirpy early morning ditty outside her window and she stirred. She went to the window to get a closer view of the warbling koel on the mango tree right outside. Her gaze wandered to her courtyard and she froze. The cornucopia of colours on her walls was stunning. She could see that they were murals, exquisitely painted, each detail in vivid relief.

She rushed downstairs and out into the patio, her hair streaming over her shoulders. She dashed to the walls to take a closer look. As she got closer, her steps faltered. She couldn't believe her eyes. These were not just innocuous, expertly drawn murals of popular goddesses. These were murals of her. The likeness was unmistakable. The fiery slant of her eyes, the haughty chin, the mole below her lip...and every line of her body seemed to be drawn with her sensuousness in mind. While at one end of the wall, she was depicted as walking away from the artist, with just a haughty look thrown over her bare shoulder and a seductive curve to her hip, at the other was an image of her lying languorously on a meadow of soft grass, a fulfilled woman, looking at the artist with desire in her eyes. All around her, Mekalai saw herself as a creature of barely contained passion. Perplexed, she blinked at the artwork. Who could have done this? Who in the world would steal into her home at night and do such a daring, cheeky thing? Even before she could think further, she knew the answer. And her cheeks turned crimson with fury. How dare he violate her privacy like this? Enough was enough, she would put an end to this.

Mekalai didn't know where to look for the man when she didn't even know his name yet, but she decided to go to the temple grounds where she had last met him. After a perfunctory search of the temple, she went outside, only to see her likeness adorning the entire length of the walls. She gasped in shock. Here he had painted her with serenity; the obvious sensuousness of the paintings on her walls had been toned down considerably. These goddesses had peace on their faces; their mysterious, sleepy smiles seemed to hold a thousand secrets. His imagination had captured Mekalai in her purest form; and as Parvathi, Lakshmi, Saraswathi, and a number of other goddesses, she saw herself as he saw her—a woman of many facets, all adored and revered. Tears stung her eyes, and utterly overwhelmed by what she was feeling, she knelt down beside the wall, her fingers grazing the paint. She hadn't planned this for sure. To be so infinitely drawn to an absolute stranger who had this kind of hold on her. She hadn't planned on feeling emotions she knew existed only in the love songs sung by travelling folk singers. She remembered Avai Paati's grand tales of love, romance, and adventure; and how she had longed to be in one of them, but this was proving altogether too difficult for her.

She felt a hand graze her shoulder and even before she had looked up, she knew who it was. That touch was unmistakable. Vikraman looked at her intently. 'Come with me,' he said quietly. She obeyed. They walked in silence through the back lanes of the town. Vikraman held her hand, leading her through innumerable turns until they came to an open ground. The sole structure there lay in ruins—a magnificent first-century temple, now ravaged by time and nature. As she looked around, taking in the beauty of the place, he took her arm and pulled her into the shade of a broken baluster with a decorative plaster canopy roof hanging precariously right above it.

'We have to talk, Mekalai,' he said.

With her back pressed against the wall behind her, and Vikraman's strong arms blocking her movement to the side, Mekalai had no choice but to look up into his eyes. She felt vulnerable and all she wanted was to be pulled into his arms. Realizing the precarious nature of her feelings, she drew on her years of aloofness and said, 'Well, maybe you could start by telling me your name.'

There was a long pause. It was as if he was contemplating telling her his name.

'See,' she rebuked, feeling her heart starting to crumble, 'you won't even tell me your name. You don't care even that much. I am just any other girl for you...' The tears threatened to flow afresh, but Mekalai didn't want to break down in front of this man. She squared her shoulders and tried to step away from the wall. 'If that is all you have to say to me, then I think we are through talking.' She tried to push past him. But Vikraman was like a rooted oak.

He had a strange gleam in his eyes. 'You're right, we are through talking.' And he silenced her in the most effective way a woman can be silenced. She closed her eyes and arched her head back slightly, willingly giving in. His tongue probed a little further in her mouth, tasting honey and her own sweet taste. She let out a little whimper. His finger traced her skin right from her cheek down to the nape of her neck. His hands rested just above her breasts. Moving his mouth away from hers, he bent his head and kissed her just at the curve of her breasts. His fingers found her nipple through her silken robes and he pinched it gently. It sprang to life at his touch. She gasped. He flicked the other nipple too, between his fingers, and she could feel her breasts straining against her robes, surprised by this sudden attention. He slowly pushed away the robe to expose a full breast crowned by its cinnamon-hued bud. He took it into his mouth and licked it gently. She arched her back, leaning against the baluster for support, still holding him close, and let out another little whimper. Then, using all the will power he could muster, he pulled himself away. She opened her eyes in surprise. They were slightly dilated with desire. She looked away, blushing furiously.

'You are not just any girl,' he said quietly. 'I feel for you what I have never felt for any woman before. But there are things I must do before I involve you in this further.'

Mekalai was suddenly angry. 'Then why bring me here, why kiss me again? Who are you anyway?'

'You must wait a little longer for that answer, unfortunately,' he said. 'But please try and trust me.'

'I'd rather die an old maid than wait for you or believe you,' she said angrily and brushed past him violently. 'And don't think a kiss or two can bind me to you. They mean nothing to me,' she continued, her tone acerbic. 'I have no use for a man who won't even tell me his name. I hope our paths will not cross again.'

With that she blazed out, and walked back quickly, not wanting him to catch up with her again. As she walked, her thoughts raced at lightning speed. How could she have even considered falling in love with someone like him? Who did he think he was? She felt like she had been played, played like a puppet in his hands, seduced by his passion and desire. All for nothing. It had ended even before it had started. Even as thunderclouds threatened to expel their fury on the earth below, her eyes were whipping up their own personal storm. She wiped away her tears violently and walked on.

Vikraman watched her go with a heavy heart. But there was little he could do at this point. He had let his primal instincts take over and had given in to his desire for this extraordinary girl. Ever since their first encounter in the woods, an indescribable bond had linked him to her. But now she was gone, and he could do nothing to stop her. He could not give her the answers she wanted, not just yet. So be it, he thought bitterly. Let the hero become the villain of the piece. I have brought this on myself...

Mekalai looked at herself in the mirror. A sullen, tormented face stared back. Guna came in with a cooling paste of sandalwood and rose water and Mekalai let her apply it to her forehead. She lay down, listening to the rain as it tattooed its presence on her roof. It was an unexpected thunderstorm and she reflected that it mirrored the one in her own life.

Reluctantly, she heaved herself out of bed after a while to get dressed to go for a betrothal feast at a neighbour's house. The last thing she wanted was to go to a place where everyone would remind her of her many elligible suitors. She wondered how many more pot-bellied merchants awaited her there. Currently she felt murderous and any idiot who dared to exasperate her today was sure to die a horrible death at her hands. For a minute Mekalai wished she was one of those flesh-eating vampires that were believed to inhabit the woods. She would have so liked to seduce that insolent stranger and then rip his throat with her bare hands and drink his blood. Her sweet face belied none of these violent thoughts, and, invitingly garbed in silk robes with matching pearl earrings, Mekalai set out towards the neighbour's mansion.

As she entered, her heart sank. The place was infested with middle-aged ladies whose staple diet was gossip. Most of them resembled large, jarigai-covered cauldrons and it seemed an unspoken rule that one had to compete actively with one another in the jewellery department. One particular lady looked like she was going to double up under the impressive weight of her adornments.

The girl whose betrothal it was had extremely large ears, a fact she tried to hide by unsuccessfully covering them with her hair. She also had hair on her chin and Mekalai heard one of the aunts whispering loudly enough for the girl's mother to hear, 'I think an apt wedding gift would be a large pumice stone, don't you think?'

The groom, who sat in the men's area, looked disinterested. The girl kept throwing covert glances at him and he seemed determined to avoid them. The ears frightened him maybe, thought Mekalai to herself wickedly. The girl's father, an unbelievably obese man famous for his miserly ways, seemed to have ballooned in proportion to his wealth and was waggling his fat hands and talking to the groom's father. Each of his fingers sported a different gem. Diamond earrings glistened in his ears. The house itself had copper pillars and lacquered flooring. Each of the seats in the receiving area was covered in imported silks and velvets. Every corner of the house screamed opulence and to Mekalai, it was just an obscene show of wealth.

'This roast pork is especially succulent,' one particularly corpulent guest informed her gleefully. She nodded politely.

'You know, they don't let the pig mate for days before its slaughter. The frustration is supposed to make its meat juicier,' he went on. Digesting this unpalatable bit of information, Mekalai smiled at him sweetly and moved away, excusing herself.

She was like a graceful, lissome swan, making every other girl in the room look distinctly pale by comparison. Needless to say, her looks had the undesired effect. She was interrupted every five minutes with a proposal from a number of men, each of whom looked less attractive than the last. Finally she went into the inner chamber where the women sat gossiping. They must have been talking about her and the unwanted effect she had on their men, because the moment she entered, an awkward hush fell over the room. She smiled at them sweetly and deliberately, then turned and left.

Craving some fresh air, she made her way up the stairs and on to the terrace. She could smell the champakam flowers in the air. The moon glistened against the purple-black sky. The calm out here seemed incongruent with the unrest inside her. She heaved a deep sigh and clutched the carved railings of the balcony. A swift movement behind her made her turn. For some reason her heart started beating wildly. She sensed a presence and before she even saw it, she knew it was the masked thief. She saw his shadowy figure outlined in the hazy light and she could see two or three more silhouettes behind him.

He is here to loot the place, she realized. Strangely, it was not fear she felt. It was a unique thrill. She had already encountered this extraordinary man. She knew he was anything but evil. Anbuselvan, whose mansion it was, had far too much wealth for his own good. It wouldn't hurt him to part with some of it.

Suddenly the masked thief turned, and he saw her. Framed against the moonlight she looked vulnerable. He went still. A moment went by while they stared at each other. For a heartbeat, Vikraman thought that she had recognized him. A small frown appeared on her forehead and she whispered, 'The thief!' Of course. She hadn't recognized the painter, but the thief whom she had met and struggled against, she knew instantly. Vikraman felt a pang of something deep in his heart as he watched her looking ethereal in the moonlit night. He walked slowly towards her, as if afraid to frighten off a rare, beautiful bird.

'Listen,' he whispered urgently, reaching her in a few strides. I want you to stay out of all this. Stay put here till you hear us leave. Is that understood?'

She nodded her head obediently. He had recognized her from the other night. She felt strangely flattered. Excitement throbbed through her veins. He motioned to the other two men with him and they made their way downstairs. She couldn't contain herself and ran to the entrance of the staircase, craning her head to hear.

She could hear his baritone issuing orders, and some screams and yelps. She could hear the women protesting hysterically even as they were being relieved of all their jewels. The men seemed oddly muted, possibly due to the sharp gleaming swords held by the bandits, and handed over their purses meekly.

The thugs began to exit the same way they had come. Pandemonium broke out on the ground floor as they saw the thugs leave and Mekalai heard Anbuselvan screaming for the town guards. But of course, the town guards were never around when one needed them, and all the miserly merchant could do was continue to bellow at the top of his voice.

Just before Vikraman climbed over the balcony of the mansion and made his way down by a rope ladder, he paused near Mekalai. She looked into those shadowy eyes and again felt a familiar stirring begin in her heart. His eyes were full of meaning. She held his gaze without flinching. He gently touched her cheek with his hand, almost wistfully, and then before she knew it, he was gone. Now she knew why people thought he wasn't real. He moved with lightning quick speed; he was almost invisible. She stared out into the darkness long after he had gone and then reluctantly made her way downstairs, where the commotion had not yet died down.

The women were in an apoplectic state. Some of them had turned an unhealthy shade of purple due to the shock and others just sat staring into space. All of them had been successfully relieved of every piece of jewellery they had been wearing.

One of them, with enormous buckteeth, stuttered, 'Did you see his bloodshot eyes? He is surely a vampire. Oh my god, we could all be dead by now.'

Mekalai who had looked into the 'vampire's' eyes quite closely and knew for a certainty that they were not bloodshot stifled a smile.

'Mekalai, you poor child, I hope they didn't harm you,' said one lady. 'What horrible times we live in. These ruffians could have done anything, they could have abducted you and and...' she trailed off faintly and sank her ample bottom on to the cushions. Mekalai rose and decided to leave before she would be subjected to more gory details of what could have been her fate at the hands of the thugs. As she left the mansion, she realized she was actually smiling. The evening had proved to be most entertaining.

Vikraman and his aides sped back on horses to the woods. This had been a highly risky but plum opportunity. Never before had they looted right inside the town. This was a first, and a satisfactory one. Nithilan was waiting impatiently for them and greeted Vikraman with profuse enthusiasm even as he disembarked from his horse. Vikraman was instantly overcome with pangs of guilt. He had spent quite some time contemplating whether he should tell Nithilan about his tryst with Mekalai. As a brother, he deserved to know, but would he approve? Would he want to see his sister with a man whose future was uncertain? And more importantly, would Mekalai want to be with him once she knew he was the masked thief? After much deliberation, he decided he would tell Nithilan. Simply because it was the right thing to do.

That night, they feasted on roasted rabbits and ducks and the newly procured foreign liquor, courtesy Anbuselvan. They drank gustily to his health. This was a time of celebration for the band of warriors. Spirits ran high in the band and Vikraman drew Nithilan away while the others made merry. Vikraman told him about the first time he had met Mekalai in the forest and how he had met her again in the town. Nithilan frowned. He said, 'Did she know you were the masked thief of Poompuhar? Do you think she will betray you? Because I urge you to believe me that she will not...I shall meet her and explain.' Vikraman stopped him from continuing and said what was uppermost in his mind—his feelings for Nithilan's sister, and how, much as he had tried, he had not been able to forget her.

Nithilan's expression turned from perplexity to disbelief to extreme wonderment. To Vikraman's utter surprise, the young man embraced him tightly, with tears rolling down his cheeks.

'Why would I not approve?' he asked between joyous sobs. 'You are the greatest man I have ever known and I think that my sister is very lucky. In fact I couldn't give her to a worthier man.'

He also offered to go to her immediately and clear the air but Vikraman objected. 'Let her find out when the time is right, and that time will soon come,' was all he had to say. Nithilan said no more.

As he lay awake under the smoky blue sky with its smattering of stars, Vikraman realized that in order to have a future with Mekalai he would have to start afresh. But before that he had some unfinished business to attend to. Things that would require all his strength and courage, he thought grimly.

Mekalai strolled in her garden because sleep continued to evade her, for the second night in a row. The faint fragrance of the flowers soothed her and the light breeze sent her hair flying softly in waves. She had had an eventful day, she reflected. She felt inexplicably sad as she thought of the stranger she had given her heart to. It was a futile exercise. She made up her mind to put it behind her but there was an ache in her heart which she knew would last forever. 'I should get some parrots,' she thought wryly. 'They will keep me company when I grow old as a spinster.'

Far in the distance, perched at the tip of Poompuhar, was the fortress that housed the tyrannical chieftain who could not get over Mekalai. Narasimhan's eyes, bloodshot with the liquor he had been consuming since the evening, gleamed with lust. He would have her before the full moon had waned. Her pesky brother had left and now she was all alone.

As he paced the murky lengths of his chamber, Narasimhan brooded over the fact that he couldn't forcibly abduct her. His reputation in the court was fragile at the moment and he wanted to take minimum risks. He had to try other tricks. He remembered Mekalai's uncle Komagan. The old fool had promised to bring Mekalai to him before long, in return for her wealth, but he seemed to have failed so far. He and that retarded son of his. 'I'll summon him tomorrow and give him one last chance,' thought Narasimhan. With that he drained his cup, threw it aside, and proceeded to his harem, to choose from the wide variety of girls held captive at his disposal.

CHAPTER SIX

THE LAST PERSON MEKALAI wanted to see at the start of the day was her uncle. She watched from her window as he skulked in through the main entrance. He looked like a vulture with his hooked nose and hunchbacked frame and she wondered how someone as angelic as her mother could have such an unpleasant sibling. She drew the bolts on the door to her room and when Guna came knocking, she emphatically told her that she would come out only after her uncle had removed himself from the premises.

When Guna informed Komagan of this, he shrugged his shoulders and simply sat down, his betel nut box by his side. He sat there chewing his paan continuously, like a cow chews its cud and finally after two hours, an exasperated and bored Mekalai gave up and went downstairs bracing herself for an unpleasant encounter.

She stood at the bottom of the stairs, leaning on the railing, arms folded. She did not want to sit down and encourage him further.

Her uncle seemed in no great hurry. He lovingly smoothened out a shrivelled, discoloured betel leaf and proceeded to put chuna on it. He then folded it multiple times and popped it into his large, yawning mouth.

Chewing slowly and deliberately, he spoke. 'Mekalai, my beloved niece, I have come to bring you to your senses...' The sharp glint in his niece's eye didn't deter him.

'Have you heard of Kadhiroli, my girl?'

Mekalai shrugged her shoulders in disinterest.

'Well, she is the mistress to Nedumaaran, the military chieftain of Thanjavur. Do you know that he has recently gifted her a necklace that has gems of every possible kind and that weighs well over a couple of kilos?'

'Does he intend to have her drowned?' asked Mekalai but the sarcasm was lost on her uncle.

He continued with utmost sincerity and an air of patience one normally bestows upon a young child. 'He has also given her a mansion that is three times the size of this one. She has twenty maids at her disposal. He gifts her diamonds, gold, and silks every other day.'

He paused for effect.

Mekalai studied her toenails. Undeterred, Komagan asked her, 'Do you understand what I mean, Mekalai?'

'Yes I do,' she said. 'Out of the door.'

Komagan clicked his tongue in exasperation. 'Try to understand, you foolish girl. Nobody is ever going to come to you with a decent proposal. Despite the handsome dowry you may be able to afford, there is no one to marry you off. Either you settle for one of those seedy merchants or you accept Narasimhan's proposal. He is very keen to have you. Trust me, Mekalai, you will live like a queen. He may treat other women like vermin, but he indulges his mistresses.'

Mekalai looked hard at her uncle, her gaze unflinching, and he began to feel uncomfortable. Finally in a very low, firm, dangerous voice, she told him to get out. He scuttled out and pausing by the doorway, left an ominous parting shot. 'You will pay the price for this, Mekalai. You are too smart for your own good.'

She took delicious satisfaction in banging the door after him. But the moment he left a dark cloud settled over her mind. She would rather choose death over relenting to Narasimhan's lewd overtures. She also reflected that he would hardly be pleased with the tidings that her uncle would bring him. And god knows what his wrath may bring. She made up her mind to go to the woods tonight and retrieve her sword from the well. She just might need it very soon...

Her day passed in languid stupor as her heart was still heavy. She walked down to Arul's house and indulged the children there by playing with their puppets and making them talk in different voices. It cheered her up a bit but she still felt despondent. Her mood did not escape Avai Paati's sharp eyes. She summoned her to her side and quickly got down to business.

'What's troubling you, my girl? Why do you

look like a wilting hibiscus? Where has all your fire gone?'

Mekalai didn't answer. She was not in a position to explain anything, least of all her encounter with the mural painter. She remained silent but this only provoked the old woman more.

'It must be the masked man then,' she said and Mekalai looked up startled.

'It must have been a shock to you, being present in the house that was burgled yesterday. Did you see the masked man? Does he really exist?'

Mekalai nodded. 'I saw him, Paati. He is real. But I don't think he is evil...' she trailed off.

Avai eyed her sharply. 'Don't you go romanticizing the thug in your heart, you foolish child. No good will come of it. In due course, I myself will find you a decent match and get you married off. Till then try and keep your errant emotions to yourself.' Mekalai nodded glumly, not wanting the old lady to press further on the subject. She returned home a little later and tried to engage herself in painting. She tried painting a likeness of the masked thief but flung the brush away after a while. Nothing seemed right just now.

In the woods, Vikraman was trying to concentrate on his carefully laid out plans. He had waited his entire life to carry this out and now a spanner in the works had arrived in the most desirable and tantalizing form. His past was so clouded that he had not even been able to tell her his name. And his silence had angered her. He reflected that while he may bypass the truth he could never blatantly lie to her. If all his plans went well, soon she would be his and he wouldn't have to be in hiding ever again. His features were grim even as he sharpened his sword on a craggy boulder.

Mekalai passed the afternoon in solitude. She had no desire to see anyone. She was waiting for the night, when she could reunite with her only source of solace.

It was around twilight that it happened. She had stepped out into the garden for a walk. Strolling around the flowery, colour-speckled place made her feel calm.

She heard a noise and turned sharply. But it was too late. A hand clamped over her mouth, and she could smell something very strange. Just before Mekalai passed out completely, she caught a glimpse of her assailant's face. Keeran's vicious features were twisted with malicious glee...

Earlier that day, Komagan had returned to his house in a state of frenzy, perplexed by his predicament. Mekalai had proved to be as stubborn as he had expected but the problem still loomed large. Narasimhan wanted her, and he had asked Komagan to convince the girl. Failure in the mission would result in a fall from grace. Convulsing slightly at the thought, he decided to employ more drastic measures.

Keeran was more than willing to oblige but only after his father had reluctantly parted with five bags of gold. He lived for this sort of diabolic pleasure and set out gleefully on his mission. Mekalai would pay for her pride, Komagan throught. She had far too much of it.

It had been easier than he had expected. She was so taken by surprise that she had hardly any time to struggle at all. Once she passed out, Keeran lifted her up and carried her to his father, who was to then go and deposit her at Manikottai. This was the easiest thing he had ever done in his whole life.

Komagan's eyes showed intense relief when he saw that his wayward son had surpassed his expectations. He immediately grabbed the reins of the chariot and sped away into the darkness.

Manikottai had a sinister air to it. It stood at the edge of a hill that overlooked the river Kaveri where it was at its turbulent best. It towered over Poompuhar in all its malevolent glory. Within its thick circular stone walls lay the palace which Narasimhan's father had built. That structure had now become the tyrant's citadel, and he had managed to infuse his own personality into every nook, cranny, and crevice.

The bastion was impenetrable. The colossal iron gates that guarded it bolted from inside. The walls, which towered over a hundred metres in height had sharp spikes on them, making it virtually impossible for anyone to climb over. Sentinels stood at every corner with sharpened spears. The entire monument was lit with a restless molten glow. It looked like a giant mass of evil, belonging to another world. And it was into the dank belly of this ill-fated monument that Komagan brought his unconscious niece.

Narasimhan's eyes had a lusty gleam. The deer had fallen into the hunter's snare at last. Tonight she would finally be his.

Back in the woods, Vikraman couldn't get Mekalai out of his mind. Yes, she had said she never wanted to see him again, but then, women said things like that. He thought of her radiance, her spirit, her courage, and he knew that he was infinitely, irreversibly in love with her. He had had many women before, women who swooned and sighed and promised everlasting love but they had, at best, been good bedmates. He thought of the prostitutes of Arikamedu, their eager, painted faces, and how all of them had professed undying love to him. He had read poetry to them lying on their seedy beds and they had sighed wistfully. He was no novice to the pleasures of the flesh and he knew exactly how to take a woman to dizzying heights of desire in his arms, but Mekalai...she was different. She had stirred up emotions he hadn't known existed, feelings he could hardly believe were so intense.

No, he must find her and tell her everything. Before embarking on his final journey for justice, he would meet the woman he loved and confess. He set off towards Poompuhar town, once again donning the innocuous persona of a young mural painter.

The room spun around as Mekalai stirred awake. Hazy shapes danced over her eyelids and she struggled with her consciousness. She felt numb and stupid, and blinked a few times, trying to comprehend her surroundings. Where was she? Had she caught some mysterious fever and was she now delirious? She half expected Guna to walk in and pull the drapes open to usher in more light. She looked around, struggling for coherence and slowly her stupor lifted. Horror descended upon her like an unwelcome thunderstorm. It washed over her in cold, clammy waves as she slowly realized where she was.

In utter panic, she looked around, hoping against futile hope that there would be a way out. But there wasn't. This must be what hell looks like, she thought. Thick black drapes swung low from the ceilings. The creepy lighting emphasized the boar and tiger heads on the walls. It was like this place had a life of its own, she thought. It was a pulsating, repulsively alive structure with the soul of its owner creeping through its stone and brick walls. She shivered, not so much from fear as from revulsion. She could not even bring herself to think about the fate that awaited her.

She got out of bed, walked towards the heavy teakwood door, and hammered on it. She pounded on it for what seemed like hours but no one came her way. It seemed like the place was devoid of any human habitation.

She flung herself back on the bed, despair rising in her heart. It would be ages before anyone realized she was missing. Guna had gone to her aunt's place and would be back only after three days. Even if her friends stopped by and found that she was not there, they wouldn't think anything was wrong until it was too late.

It seemed ages before she even heard a sound. The massive doors creaked open and an elderly maid walked in with a deadpan expression.

'You are to get ready,' she said and handed her a set of crimson red silk robes and plenty of gold jewellery.

'Whatever for?' yelled Mekalai. 'Why should I get ready, for what? I demand to be sent home now!'

Her screaming seemed to have no effect on the maid at all, as she shrugged her shoulders and said, 'As you please. The master will come by soon.'

Mekalai threw the robes at the maid who caught them deftly. Clearly she was used to behaviour of this sort from abducted girls, reflected Mekalai dryly.

After the maid's departure, Mekalai searched every nook and corner of the room for a way to escape. There was none. There were two large windows overlooking the main gate and it was a steep drop to the ground. It was pitch dark outside and she knew Poompuhar must have retired for the night. No one in that town would miss her.

Mekalai felt nauseous at the thought of what

awaited her. It wouldn't be long before Narasimhan would come to prey on her like a beast of the wild. Now she knew how Sita must have felt when Ravana abducted her.

To her surprise, nobody came that night again to disturb her. Narasimhan was displaying an uncharacteristic show of patience, she thought. After what seemed like ages, she fell into a troubled sleep, dreaming of a masked man on a black stallion, and a mural painter who had his eyes. When dawn crept in reluctantly she awoke. Again, a sea of panic washed over her. The night had passed and although she was as safe as she could be under the circumstances, she was still here, in Manikottai, a prisoner to the lust of a tyrannical demon. The fortress seemed less ominous in daylight but it still didn't look like a happy place. She went to the window and looked out. It was the same sun and the same cloud-spotted sky but it just didn't seem as beautiful from where she was standing. Everything seemed dark and hopeless. A maid came in with some fruit and milk. She ate the fruit hungrily.

In the afternoon the maid returned, offering to bathe Mekalai, and she agreed. She let the maid oil her hair and rub her body with an aromatic paste of sandalwood, turmeric, and some strange exotic herbs. The bath refreshed her. She dressed in the robes laid out and lay down on the bed. In the evening the maid returned with the same clothes, instructions, and deadpan expression. Once again, Mekalai threw the robes back at her, flung the jewellery out of the door, and told her to get out.

After what seemed aeons, the door burst open. If Yama truly existed, this is what he would have looked like, thought Mekalai. Narasimhan barged in like a mad bull. His eyes were bloodshot and steeped in fury, and his massive nostrils were flared. The moustache that extended generously from one end of his face to the other bristled. He seemed at least six feet taller than Mekalai. His voice thundered across the expanse of the room. She shrank back in terror.

'What the hell do you mean you won't get ready? Do you take me for a fool? You are here, in Manikottai. Here you do as I tell you. I have been putting up with your tantrums for too long. I am losing my patience.'

Mekalai stood rooted to the spot, paralysed with fear. He took note of her quivering form and his gaze lingered longer on her breasts. He was undressing her mentally, she thought. He was stripping away every piece of clothing on her. She felt disgusted, violated, and helpless.

Suddenly his demeanour changed. He let out a little chortle. 'I had planned such a big surprise for you and you had to ruin it by being your stubborn self. You see, I have had a small change of mind. I've decided to marry you and then ravish you to my heart's content. I have too many abductions to my name and I think a respectable marriage will help my reputation considerably. So this is the schedule—you be nice, get into the bridal finery I sent and I shall see you at the mandapam.'

Seeing her expression, he added, 'Don't worry, there is a priest there and he will perform the rites legally. I mean to do this. Tonight you will be mine!'

She spat in his face. It took all her courage to do it, but her inner fire would not take this lying down. The look of astonishment on his face lasted for a flicker of a second. Anger pulsated through his face but he made an effort to control it. His eyes spewed lust as he leered at her. He took a step forward and grabbed her by the hair. Her eyes darted furiously, fearfully. He kissed her with brutal force. He could feel her writhing violently under him and he cupped one of her buttocks with his hand. She could feel the strength of his thighs pressing against her. He planted hot harsh kisses on her face, forehead, in the little ravine that ran between her perfectly shaped breasts. His hands roamed all over her and Mekalai fought him helplessly, trying to push him away with all her might. With brutal force he held on to her, impressing his strength on her body. She tried to put up a fight but Narasimhan was too strong for her. He held on to her the way a fisherman holds on to his flapping, convulsing catch. He pushed her against the wall and tugged at her robes. She let out an anguished cry. His lips were still hot on her body.

There was a knock on the door and he finally let her go, throwing her back, so she fell on the ground in a crumpled heap. 'That was the appetizer. A taste of things to come. And if you behave yourself, it might work out better for you.'

With that he stormed out, leaving Mekalai in a distraught puddle of tears, anger, and grief. This time when the maids came, she was reticent. She let them bathe her in perfumed water, dab her with ittar, douse her hair and her body in fragrant fumes from exotic herbs and leaves. She dressed in the red robes he had sent for her. She left her hair loose as a mark of defiance and wouldn't allow the maid to fix a band of jasmine and roses around her tresses. Finally, she told them she wished to be alone for a while before she went down to the mandapam. The maids exchanged quick glances, and one of them spoke up. 'But Master has asked us not to leave you alone.'

'I am not one of those cheap prostitutes your master is used to hoarding here. I am now going to be mistress of this house. You better get used to obeying my commands.'

The ruse worked. The maids, totally taken aback by her suddenly feudal air, backed out of the room in quick succession. Once they had left, Mekalai looked around the room frantically. She needed something, even a stick would do, as long as she could at least attempt to protect her honour. Her eyes fell on the bowl of fruit and the tiny gold peeling knife lying beside it, and she pounced on it. It wasn't much but it would have to do. She didn't want to dwell on the futility of her actions, how ineffectual her attempt to salvage her dignity tonight would be. She would try with all her might. The vision of Narasimhan's weight on her body on the nuptial bed made her sick. She would not let that happen.

She left the chamber and headed up the colossal wooden staircase with its gold railings, to the terrace. As she walked up, she caught a glimpse of herself in a gold mirror on the stairway. She had seen goats, decorated with garlands and vermilion, dragged away to be sacrificed in yajnas organized to appease the gods. The creatures could sense what was going to happen to them. They could smell the impending doom. She had looked into their eyes and sensed their despair. She felt like that—a creature to be sacrificed at the altar of everything that was wrong with the world. She felt around for the little gold knife, with its useless blunt edge, hidden in the folds of her robes. She would fight tooth and nail till the end.

Her thoughts, as she wound her way around the seemingly never-ending ascent to hell, slowly turned to the masked thief and the mural painter. Somehow she was unable to think of them as two different people any more. She had felt a strong, though brief, attraction towards the thief that night in the woods. For the first time, her body had come alive as a woman that day. And then her tryst with the mural painter only reinforced it. She had learnt what desire really was. She had felt complete in his arms, she now admitted. She remembered his hot passionate kisses that had urgency and tenderness all at once, and she remembered how his hand had felt on her exposed breast, how his lips had pronounced her name as they travelled down the valley of her breasts. She had fallen in love with him, his easy charm, his magnetism, and she had wanted to trust him instinctively. But now it was too late. She had given her heart to a man she would never really know and now, could never have.

She had reached the top of the stairs. The entrance to the terrace was painted in black and gold with floral flutings and sordid cherubs with horns in their mouths. Some architect who must have travelled to Greece had imposed his half-baked knowledge of its magnificent architecture on this entrance.

The place looked like it had been readied for a funeral, not a wedding. The wedding mandapam had been arranged in a hurry by a bevy of surprised attendants. There was not a soul in sight save for Narasimhan and a scrawny priest who looked like he was going to pass out. Desolation hung heavy in the air, as Mekalai took slow, unhurried steps towards the pandal. Narasimhan towered over her, like an ogre with lust-addled eyes.

Mekalai closed her eyes. This is the end, she thought. The end of my life as I know it. Never had she imagined she would be so helpless. Narasimhan impatiently pulled her up the stone steps on the mandapam, where an apologetic fire burnt and the even more sorry-looking priest began to mumble his ritualistic chants.

'Enough of this gibberish. Just get on with the ceremony,' growled Narasimhan and Mekalai's hand instinctively flew to her waist where she had concealed her ineffective weapon. She longed for her sword more than she had ever longed for it just now. The priest scrambled to his feet and placed a garland in each of their hands. The flowers, too, felt dead and clammy against her palm. This cannot be happening, she thought. It really cannot.

It happened with the sudden shock of a meteor shower. She saw someone on the parapet, who possessed the agility of a mountain leopard. As he sprang up on the parapet, his silhouette framed against the dark of the night, she gasped.

He had come for her, she really had come for her.

Or had he? This was too much of a coincidence... or was it?

CHAPTER SEVEN

In that split second, a thousand questions raced through her mind. How had this happened? How did he know she was here? Her amazement slowly turned to relief and then in turn, evolved into a tingling sensation of thrill and drama. From then on, everything was a blur. She could see that he had not come alone. He had at least ten men with him. They circled Narasimhan as he let out a thundering roar and grabbed Mekalai roughly, drawing her closer to him. She instinctively unearthed the little gold knife and plunged it into his shoulder. Narasimhan swerved blindly, more from the shock than the pain. His eyes pierced through her, sending a shiver down her spine. He let out a fearful roar of agony and in that second, when he was too blinded by pain to keep his hold on her, she freed herself. The masked thief darted forward and swung her around in his arms. She was rendered breathless, for some reason other than excitement.

'Are you all right?' he asked quietly. She nodded, her eyes never leaving his shrouded face.

One of his men dashed forward towards them

and when Mekalai turned to face him, she realized who it was. Nithilan, her brother. She could see his eyes brimming over with emotion and she instantly recognized him even though his face was covered. They looked at each other but before they could say anything, Vikraman let out an animal-like war cry and struck down a guard who was about to knife them.

More guards poured in. They rained their blows ruthlessly and without much skill, as most of them failed to even scratch their agile opponents. Vikraman fenced and deflected blows. Swords screeched as they clashed against one another forcefully.

Mekalai saw how Nithilan neatly evaded a spear that could have passed right through his chest. She stood there in the middle of all the action, watching in frenzy and fascination. She looked around warily for her abductor and saw him striding furiously towards her.

Narasimhan's eyes blazed with hellish fury. His shoulder still had the little knife embedded in it, and blood stained his arms and robes. He pulled out the knife savagely. He drew out his sword and lashed it out against her. It barely grazed her hair as Vikraman pulled her out of the way. Suddenly the thundering of footsteps sounded on the staircase and within seconds, another deluge of armed guards stormed in on to the terrace. Mekalai gasped. There were too many. They charged with their swords at Vikraman and his men, who parried and countered the attack ruthlessly for what seemed like ages. Vikraman still held on tightly to Mekalai even as he skilfully warded off the assailants. Suddenly Narasimhan was nowhere to be seen. One by one the guards fell, proving to be no match for the bandit's skilful swordsmanship.

As the last one fell, Vikraman motioned to his men to exit the way they had come.

'I will follow with her, go on!' he urged. Nithilan hesitated and then turned towards the parapet but not without a reassuring backward glance at his sister.

To Mekalai's utter horror, she heared more steps advancing up the staircase. She looked at Vikraman wildly and he pulled her behind a baluster for safety.

'We will be outnumbered. There is no way you can fight an army of guards on your own,' she said, her voice trembling with panic.

His sharp eyes bore into her and something within her stirred—an unmistakably familiar feeling. But before she could dwell on it, Narasimhan's voice thundered in the surroundings. He was murderous. He wanted the intruder's blood and he wanted his errant bride back. Mekalai heard him bark out vicious orders. 'Kill that thug but bring me the girl,' he bellowed.

'Listen, from now on, don't think, don't speak. Just do as I tell you,' Vikraman instructed Mekalai, his tone urgent. His voice had fortitude which comforted her. He looked strong, dependable, and valiant. She nodded, her eyes widening in apprehension, and he added softly, 'And trust me.'

With that, he steered her towards the other end of the terrace and just as she was wondering where he was going, a little trapdoor seemed to materialize, almost out of nowhere, in the farthest corner of the wall.

'I hope it still works,' muttered Vikraman as he slid the heavy bolt back and ushered Mekalai in first.

Total darkness. It engulfed her like a black storm, taking her breath away. She felt like it had clutched her throat, strangling her even as her eyes fought furiously with the murky space, trying to fathom where they were. She sought Vikraman's hand instinctively and he locked his fingers with hers. It was a reassuring feeling.

'There are steps here,' he whispered. 'Just hold my hand and I will guide you.'

'But how do you know,' she began, when he cut her off.

'We can talk later. Let's go now.'

The staircase seemed to go on forever and after a while, Mekalai's steps started to falter. Vikraman helped her climb the spiralling steps and she thought she was going to be dizzy from going round and round. Then finally when she thought she just couldn't go on, she spotted a sliver of light. They were at the end of the passage. It turned to a narrow corner and at the end of the damp stone wall was a tiny window.

Vikraman looked at the young girl next to him and said, 'Down below flows the Kaveri where it is at its turbulent best. This is our only chance. Are you ready for this?' She nodded her head. She had to trust this man. She had no other choice and something deep in her heart told her she had not placed her faith in the wrong man.

They climbed on to the narrow ledge of the window. She could see the water gushing far below them and she realized where she was. At the tip of Manikottai, its highest point, where it seemed dangerously perched right at the edge of the craggy hillscape.

The water looked rough and merciless. This wasn't the calm water that flowed quietly at the edges of Poompuhar. This wasn't the water in the serene bathing blocks where she and her friends had splashed around. This was the Kaveri in her most fearful, magnificent form, just before she surrendered to the wild desires of the sea.

The wind whipped up a storm around them. Mekalai's hair fluttered wildly, wrapping around her neck like a dark cape. She tucked in her upper robe so she wouldn't lose it in the gale. She closed her eyes, trying not to think of the swirling waters.

When she opened her eyes again, the shroud had lifted from the masked thief's face. The wind had carried it away and along with it, his secret persona. The world stopped. She forgot about the tumultuous waters down below, the sharp rocks, the rapids that could tear them to pieces. She stared into the face, the eyes that had perplexed her, the mouth that had taunted her, kissed her, the nose with its strong, aristocratic slant. And finally she saw his soul. It glittered like a star and she was enveloped in its radiance. This was the man she had given her heart to, the only man she had ever desired. There weren't two different men. The masked thief was also the man who had painted her dreams. Her love was finally whole, complete. She searched deep inside her own soul and realized that this was the truth she had always known. His eyes twinkled, and then in the next instant, he caught her by the waist and jumped into the swirling currents below.

The water hit them like a cold, hard slab of stone. The moon's hazy, distorted reflection travelled with them all the way. The rapids were massive and they were carried along at whatever speed the current took them. Mekalai flailed her arms around attempting to swim, but Vikraman reached out to stop her. The water was too forceful; it was no use. He held on to her with all his might, keeping her head above the water. Finally, after what seemed like aeons, the water seemed calmer. The landscape came into view and Mekalai took in the dense, dark foliage that fringed the banks. With a jolt, she realized that these were the woods. The forest that she felt belonged to her. They were at the darkest end of it, the side that possibly no one had ever ventured into. No boats came this way as the rocks were too treacherous. Finally, gasping for breath, they swam with all their force towards the banks. The blinding darkness shrouded them and the moon seemed just a distant dim lantern in the distance. They managed to pull themselves up on the bank. Wet, struggling for breath, and overcome with exhaustion, they lay down beside each other, their fingers intertwined.

They stayed like that for what seemed like hours. Finally Vikraman sat up. Mekalai turned to look at him. He gazed into her impossibly beautiful face and tenderly, very slowly, traced the mole beneath her lip. She shivered, a little at his touch and a little because of the cold.

'Let's find some shelter,' he said. 'My hideout is too far from here and you will not be able to walk. We can go there tomorrow.'

As they faced the thick darkness of the woods together, Mekalai felt more alive than she had ever felt. Her senses were so acutely tuned she thought she could hear the grasshoppers clicking their wings and the lizards in deep conversation. Owls hooted in the distance. She felt life quiver under her feet and she was certain that the tall trees were speaking to her, taking her name. The deathly stillness of the night too seemed to have a melody of its own, and as she walked hand in hand with the man she had given her heart to, she realized she had never felt happier. She was also increasingly aware of how soaked she was, how her robes were in tatters, and how each glide, each line, each curve of her body was apparent.

Vikraman walked steadily and quietly next to her, guiding her over gnarled roots and sharp-edged stones. His face betrayed none of the emotions surging through him. Passion teased him, set him on fire as he led this goddess through the glade. He longed to feel her soft lips against his, her sweet breath upon his face.

Finally they came to a little alcove with some dry sand and trees with branches hanging low. The stars sparkled with their nightly glow right above.

'We'll stop here for the night,' said Vikraman.

While Mekalai sat, shivering slightly, her damp robes sticking to her skin, he lit a small fire. She watched him expertly rub the stones together till the flames flickered to life. Soon, the fire created a comforting warmth and Mekalai put her hands out to warm them.

Vikraman sat down next to her. To him, it seemed her eyes held a million questions, all at once. And she wanted answers. He would tell her everything, even secrets of his past that he had shared with none, but right now, he felt the pangs of desire surging through him. The questions would have to wait. So would the world and everything else in it. Right now, he could hold out no more...

He sensuously flicked her wet robes off her shoulders. The action was so tantalizing, with his fingers brushing lightly against her soft skin, that Mekalai shivered with pleasure. He edged behind her and slowly undid the knots of the cloth that she had wrapped around her chest. The garment fell off her sculpted bosom and he gently, firmly, cupped her full breasts. She arched her neck back and sighed. He kissed her swiftly and deeply, and she opened her mouth to taste him, brushing his lips with her tongue. The world seemed to spin at a dizzying speed as they kissed passionately, he calling out her name and she moaning in response. Her body melted under his scorching touch.

Vikraman felt like he would drown in this sea of passion and desire. He broke the kiss and travelled downwards, planting kisses on her throat, shoulders, and the perfect valley of her full, firm breasts. He bent his head and circled one dark aureole with the tip of his tongue, all the while rubbing the other with his fingers. She gasped in ecstasy and he sucked deeply, lightly grazing his teeth over her while she clenched her teeth in a frenzy of passion. His hands caressed her, explored her with a tenderness and passion she hadn't imagined even in her wildest dreams.

He gently bit her nipples, evoking a cry from her. He pushed her back urgently, he could feel his manhood rising and knew he couldn't hold out much longer. He tugged roughly at her lower robes and they fell apart gracefully, revealing her tiny waist, the utterly tantalizing, perfectly indented belly button, her long legs, and the deep, deep heaven of pleasure between them. He kissed and nipped his way down to her belly. He put his tongue inside the little concave button and she arched back even more in pleasure. He teased her, brought her to the brink of madness by hovering just above the shiny, untouched tuft between her creamy thighs. Finally when she thought she couldn't bear it any more, he moved his mouth down across the slope of her belly and into the little curls that hid her womanhood, kissing her there. She laced her fingers through his hair, white heat exploding inside her even as he moved his tongue expertly in circles. She cried out and he looked up. He moved back to her waiting breasts and licked them. He could feel a torrent of desire surging through him and he knew he couldn't control himself any more. He crushed his lips against hers, kneading her soft lips with his. He parted her legs and slid a gentle finger inside feeling around for her gossamer soft virginity. He pushed against it gently and she moaned. Gently, he eased himself into her and she let out a cry. She lost her mind, writhing with pleasure under him as he stroked her, slowly at first and then with increasing urgency. She clawed at him, pressing her hips against him, arching her back as he kissed her neck. He rocked inside her and she moved with him in perfect rhythm as he thrust deeper inside her, changing her irreversibly from girl to woman. They became an erotic rainbow of light as they melded into each other, as if to become one, and the light burst into a million rays, sending shivers of unbridled pleasure and passion coursing through them. Desire mounted sky high like a volcano and they came together in clenching, sweltering spasms. Heat coursed through them like fiery lava and he called out her name and brought her to the denouement with him, with a shattering, throbbing operatic joy.

They lay, exhausted and exhilarated, crumpled in each other's arms on the velvety grass. The moon, stars, and sky seemed to meld into one under the heat of their overwhelming passion. Finally he moved, pulling her closer and she nuzzled his neck, content. She absently traced the scar on his arm, the one he had hidden with a bandage. Before she could ask him about it, her senses dulled with exhaustion and her eyes started to close. She is a miracle, he thought. A miracle sent down from the heavens just for me. I'll never be done with her, I'll never have enough. One night was not enough, one lifetime would fall short. He wanted a million more and then thought even that would fall short. 'I want her till the end of eternity,' he thought.

Her eyes closed in slow slumber. He watched her sleep. She was like a dewdrop, a dewdrop laced with fire. And what fire, oh god. He recalled how she had instinctively responded to his touch, her virgin moves pleasuring him more than any woman he had ever had. He gazed at her dark hair, glistening like a river on the grass. He watched her soft lips part and sigh. He curled up against her, holding her close and joined her in a sweet, dreamless sleep.

Night gave way to day and when it came streaming through the gleaming trees, Mekalai stirred. Her body felt different. It spoke to her in a new language and the memories of the night before surged through her mind. She felt herself blushing and smiling and when she turned to look at the beautiful man beside her, her heart pounded painfully with the force of love. She got up, pulling her robes around her, leaving him fast asleep, spreadeagled on his back.

She washed herself in the river, singing a little song

to herself. The universe seemed harmonious, perfect. Every sound, every texture, every hue of light and dark seemed woven together in an intricate patchwork of happiness.

She waded out of the water and sat on the shore. Last night had turned her life around forever. Things would never be the same again. Her old life had vanished along with the night, and even though she was uncertain about what the future held for her, she was absolutely certain of where her heart, soul, and body belonged. This was the kind of story the nomadic bards wrote about and now it had happened to her. She thought of her lover and suddenly with a jolt, she realized she didn't know his name yet. The masked thief and the mural painter was still nameless to her. It never occurred to her to ask him while they were in the throes of passion the previous night. And this realization brought a hundred questions to her mind. True, he had come for her, perhaps at the behest of her brother, but did he love her? He was the masked thief of Poompuhar, that was what he did—help people who needed him.

The passion she had felt last night, the intensity was unmistakable but she had no proof that he really *loved* her. To want her body was one thing but to love her was entirely different. She was intelligent enough to know the difference between the two. She thought about last night, his smouldering passion, his masculinity inside her, his kisses, and how she had writhed, moaned, responded to his every touch. She wanted him again but did he? She may have granted him one night of pleasure and she may have even engaged him for a while but love was another ball game. Women give their hearts too easily, she thought.

She wandered around in the shady glade for a while. Was last night just a fleeting dream, never to recur? Or would her instincts prove right? Would he love her as much as she loved him? She knew now that she could belong to no other, she would never be able to lie in bed with another man and let him touch her. She played for keeps. And this extraordinary man with all his secrets was linked to her destiny.

When Vikraman arose, he looked around for Mekalai. The trees exhaled a woody scent that he loved and the birds were twittering merrily. Everything seemed so perfect. His heart was knitted into a strange pattern of emotions. He had found the woman he wanted to spend the rest of his life with, but he couldn't tell her that. He had to hold back, show restraint until he had accomplished his ultimate goal. He had waited all his life for it. He loved her, but he could not tell her just yet, he realized with a pang of pain. He could not tell her until everything had become all right. Dragging her into his worries was unfair. She was protected by her innocence. And he would continue to protect her even if it meant hurting her for the present.

He got up and walked towards the banks, hoping to find her there. He saw her glistening in the sunshine, sitting gracefully near a hovering butterfly. It fluttered around her and she laughed, a perfect melody to his ears, her hair fluttering in the perfumed breeze. She seemed ethereal. She looked like an apsara from the sky. They do descend on earth occasionally, they do, he thought, to seduce men and cast an eternal spell on them.

She turned, feeling his gaze, her eyes flecked with light. And she smiled. He ran towards her and swooped her up in a passionate embrace. Their lips met and alternating between tenderness and urgency, they kissed for a while. She ran her hands over his hard torso and back. He let his hands roam all over her. They stayed locked in a sensuous embrace for a while and then gently, he let her go. She stood back, her eyes glazed with passion, her hair streaming around her face. He pushed back the errant locks and gazed into her questioning eyes. She was a temptress, a witch, he thought. She couldn't be real.

'Will you tell me your name now?' she asked almost coyly.

He told her. She said it aloud. 'Vikraman.' He smiled.

'How did you find me? How did you know that Narasimhan had had me abducted?' she asked curiously.

He pulled her into the shade and they sat down by the trunk of an enormous banyan tree, its snaky tendrils hanging low, touching the ground in various places.

'I wanted to have a glimpse of you again. I wanted to talk to you. The thought that I would never see you again, or hold you in my arms, was killing me. I went to your house that night in the hope that I could see you but you didn't seem to be there. That got me thinking. When I came back here, I told Nithilan that you were missing. He was beside himself with worry. He was sure Narasimhan had something to do with it. Some discreet enquiries at the taverns told us that Komagan had been to see Narasimhan the previous night. It didn't take us long to put two and two together. Some gentle words with Keeran which resulted in two broken teeth and a bloody nose for him, and we knew exactly where we could find you,' he finished with a laugh.

Before she could say anything he said passionately, 'Mekalai, I will tell you everything about myself. Every single thing. But now is not the time. I lead a perilous life and the less you know about it, or me, the better for you. Right now, no one connects me to you except for the fact that I rescued you. But that's what I do. It is expected of me, the bandit of Poompuhar.'

She took a step back and he caught her wrist.

'Listen to me,' he said hoarsely. 'It is a lot more complicated than you think. And I want you to be able to go back to the town and lead a respectable life. No, I cannot allow you to live in the woods with me. This life is not suitable for a woman and besides, it's too dangerous.'

He cupped her troubled face in his hands and said, 'Please trust me...give me some time. I will tell you everything. But there are things I must do, and the less you know about it, the better for you.'

Mekalai's exquisite features were drawn into a perplexed frown.

'We will lie low here in the forest for the next few days,' Vikraman continued. 'We will go to my hideout today. When the dust has settled a little bit in Poompuhar, I will smuggle you out. You can't return to your town, at least not right now. I will take you to Arikamedu where you will be safe. I have connections there.'

She understood the sincerity in his voice, his imploring tone, and decided that she would trust him, implicitly. He still hadn't said that he loved her, or that he even had serious feelings for her but she pushed that thought out of her mind. Her curiosity would have to wait. Besides, she reflected, she really had nothing to lose.

They spent the morning in peaceful solitude. They plucked fruit from the trees and sucked on their succulent juices. He picked wild flowers and made a vibrant wreath for her hair. In the afternoon he went a little deeper into the woods and caught two rabbits. He skinned them before he showed them to Mekalai, and even though she was a little distressed, hunger prevailed and the rabbits were soon smoking over the fire. Vikraman scoured the trees for herbs that could be used to enhance the meat. He crushed the leaves with his hands and applied the paste to the roasting meat.

Hunger appeased, they lay down in the shade and made slow, languorous love. Mekalai lay in his arms, her lips swollen and bruised from the kissing and her eyes dilated with love and desire.

She was throwing caution to the winds, she decided. But what was life if it didn't involve a few risks?

Vikraman decided to find his hideout a little before sundown. He had never been this far in the woods but the compass in his head told him which direction to head to.

She would be safer there, he reflected. A couple of days there and he would let destiny unfold. The time had come...

CHAPTER EIGHT

THE DARKEST CORE OF the woods was also the most beautiful and serene. It took them a day to find it but Vikraman, with his keen sense of direction, had little trouble. These woods had been his home for a few years now and he felt like they knew him as well he knew them.

Vikraman's hideout was nothing like what Mekalai had expected. It was just an enclosure with a protective shroud of trees. There was practically nothing there except for some thatched hutments and a few cauldrons strewn around the place. There was not a soul around. Most of his men, he explained, lived double lives. They spent their day in the town, mingling with the crowds as usual, but by night, they became his comrades.

Mekalai looked around for her brother but he was nowhere in sight. 'He must have gone to Kanchipuram. There are some merchants there who need help with lightening their load of wealth. He must have gone there to mark the times when their merchandise comes in.' Something in his voice made her look up. There was bitterness there, just the slightest tinge, and anger.

'It's not wrong to be rich,' she said.

'It's not wrong, but these are men who trampled on others' happiness to get what they want. I abhor people like that. Greed corrupts. It destroys lives. People who let it take over their lives deserve to get their due.' As he said this, his face burnt with an aristocratic hue. He had the air of a young, earnest king, keen to dispense justice. Mekalai felt warmth course through her body as she listened to him.

The day passed lazily. Mekalai washed her soiled, torn robes in the river and when she appeared in front of him, dressed in his substitute robes, his eyes twinkled.

Even the heavy robes he had loaned her didn't hide the luscious curves of her body and he drew her close with a groan. His lips locked with hers in urgency and his hands moved to find her breasts. She moulded herself into him willingly submitting to his caresses and kissing him back intensely.

'Mekalai, I never thought I could feel this way about any woman,' he whispered as he nibbled her ear.

She pulled away suddenly and he was amused and exasperated by the look of jealousy on her face.

'Exactly how many women have you been with?' she asked a little sullenly, her full lips curling into a pout.

He scanned her face with an amused grin playing around his mouth and then said in a perfectly serious voice, 'Enough to make you jealous.'

She got up, pulling the robes around her.

'Well, clearly your romantic life has been quite prolific. Any old flames I should be wary of?'

He stretched lazily on the grass and drawled, 'Tsk tsk, Mekalai, jealousy doesn't become you...come back into my arms...'

But she wouldn't. He had once again evaded her queries, and was now being vague and offhand. Maybe I am just a passing fancy, she thought. He is enticed by my body. Once he tires of that...The thought depressed her.

Women are always so stupid, she thought. Fall in love first, ask questions later. Why should a man like him want to be bound by a girl like me...

She wandered off, traversing through the woods, listening to the birds sing their sweet melodies, hidden from view. In contrast to the brick-and-plaster marvel that was Poompuhar, the woods were like a divine island. Mekalai felt she was all alone here, complete in her solitude. It seemed impossible that any man had ever set foot inside it...she felt one with it. Not for the first time in her life, she felt that this was her home, her secret haven, and she could see why Vikraman had chosen this place as his stronghold.

She suddenly thought of her sword. It pierced through her like a bolt of lightning that she could easily retrieve her sword now. She sprinted across the woods until she reached the fringes. The well looked like it had been waiting for her all this while. She deftly climbed down it and crawled into the little opening where she normally hid her sword. It was there, shrouded in black oilcloth. She unearthed it and the blade gleamed like a jewel in her hands. She stuck it in her robes near her hip and started to climb her way back out. She heard a rustling in the bushes and she had a distinct feeling of déjà vu. She paused at the rim of the well like a deer that has sensed its stalker. Her keen sense of hearing told her that an intruder was around and she felt instinctively that he was not friendly.

She crept out of the well in silence and noiselessly drew her sword from its sheath. Her eyes scanned the woods, sharply tuned to catch even the slightest movement. Sensing a presence behind her, she turned swiftly and looked right into the eyes of a young man. He had a dagger that he clutched tightly in his hand, and his face showed a frantic sense of purpose. He moved towards her, his weapon at a threatening angle and suddenly he lunged forward in a distinct motion of attack.

Totally prepared for it, she swung around to avoid his attack and thrust her sword at him. A mere dagger was no match for her sword, she thought, but this man was a lot stronger than her. One wrong move and she would easily be overpowered. They fenced, circling each other. She didn't take her eyes off his face once and once or twice she thought she saw fear and trepidation in it. In an unexpected move, with a smart flick of her sword, she managed to remove his shroud. The scarf fell to reveal a very young man, his expression fearful. She brought the tip of her sword to rest on the pulsating nerve on his neck and asked quietly, 'Who are you?'

'I...I thought you were about to attack me,' he stammered, his eyes darting wildly to the steely edge on his neck.

'You are lying, tell me who you are and why you attacked me.'

Her mind raced furiously. He looked vaguely familiar. One of the youth at the town square perhaps. And if he was in the woods wearing a shroud...what were the odds?

She decided to take a dangerous chance.

'Are you aligned with the masked thief?' she asked boldly.

The question caught him unawares and he looked totally aghast.

'I...yes,' he stuttered.

She gave him a long, hard look. His face was weak, his chin had no character. His eyes were diffident. It was difficult to believe that Vikraman would have chosen such a man to join his gang. The young man flinched a little as she drove the edge of the sword a little deeper into his skin.

'I don't believe you. Lay down your puny dagger. It stands no chance against my sword.'

He dropped the dagger to the ground and it fell with a soft clang. She relaxed her stance.

'We'll settle this once and for all. I am going to take you to your leader. If he doesn't recognize you,

you can be certain you will be revolving neatly on the barbeque spit tonight.'

She saw his eyes flicker with fright. She asked him to walk ahead with his hands above his head and she walked a few paces behind him, her sword still drawn. As they entered the darker peripheries of the forest, she relaxed a little. He seemed to know the way to the hideout. This must be one of Vikraman's men, she thought. But she didn't like the look of him.

A deer darted past her, and she was momentarily distracted by the blur of motion. It was her undoing. Her assailant swooped down on the opportunity and swerved around, hitting her square in the jaw. She was thrown to the ground by the impact and her sword flung far from her.

The man loomed large over her, his eyes now gleaming with vehement malice.

'There is a price of ten thousand ingots for the man who takes you back to Narasimhan. Ten thousand ingots for a mere chit of a girl,' he leered. 'You must be very special to him.'

She tried to inch away from him, horror washing over her.

'I didn't lie. I am one of Vikraman's men. But I am tired of this life. I am tired of his "goodness", his "nobility", his thirst for "justice". I joined the league hoping to make some quick money. But these fools here, the last thing they are really interested in is money. We bring back sacks and sacks of spoils, enough to fill the king's treasury, risking our lives for it, and what do we do? We give it all away,' he spat bitterly. 'It was a stroke of luck for me, wasn't it, that I spotted you on the way back from the town? I can leave these damned woods forever and start afresh with the money you will so kindly help me obtain. Vikraman and his crusade against the rich be damned.'

He proceeded to untie a length of rope from around his waist and Mekalai looked around hastily, hoping for some chance of escape. He was unarmed; his dagger had been left behind near the well and he hadn't thought of picking up her sword. It lay gleaming, half hidden among the tall blades of grass. She needed a second, a split second.

As he drew closer with the rope, she writhed away from him on the ground, steering away from the grassy patches to the more muddy ones. It had to be done now, not a second later.

Suddenly she looked behind the man and let out a blood-curdling scream and he looked around seized with panic. She gathered some mud together in a sweeping move and hurled it towards his face. The man backed away wildly, blinking furiously, momentarily blinded by her clever action.

Mekalai got to her feet and rushed to pick up her sword. Not wasting another second, she bolted deep into the forest, wanting to get as far away from her attacker as possible. The trees seemed a blur as she raced past them without a backward glance. She collided headlong with Vikraman and he caught her roughly.

'What happened? he demanded. 'I heard a scream.'

Gasping for breath, pushing her hair away from her face, she told him briefly what had happened.

'Stay here,' he instructed her. And before she could stop him, he was gone. Despite the authority in his voice, she was unable to hold herself back and she ran after him.

When she found him, he was standing over the assailant in the clearing. The tip of his sword was pinned to the man's gut. For a second she thought that he had killed the man. But then she saw him move and she breathed a sigh of relief. Stricken by the fear of certain death, the man was making spluttering sounds. Vikraman looked angrier than Mekalai had ever seen him.

'You! I knew it was a mistake to include you in my fold in the first place. You have always displayed weakness. But your eagerness got the better of me. You deserve to die, you scum of the earth,' he said and swung his blade with force when Mekalai dashed to stop him.

'Don't!' she beseeched. 'Don't. He doesn't deserve to die by your hands.' Vikraman's blazing eyes met her anguished ones and he relented.

'Till I decide what is to be done with you, I'll let you stay here bound to this tree,' he said, hoisting the man roughly up on his feet and winding the length of the rope around him. He bound him tightly to a mango tree and tied his mouth with a rag. They made their way back into the woods, leaving him there.

Vikraman was lost in thought as they walked back. She could sense his turmoil but she walked beside him in silence. When they reached the hideout, Vikraman said, 'You are not safe here any more. I must send you away.'

'I am not going anywhere!' she argued angrily. 'I am staying here with you and my brother.'

'Don't be a fool, Mekalai,' he said impatiently. 'Your brother can take care of himself and as for me, a life riddled with peril is what I have chosen for myself. I will not hear another word. Tomorrow I myself will take you somewhere safe and you can stay there till I...till this whole thing settles down. Narasimhan will hopefully tire of looking for you.'

'You think I can't take care of myself,' she shouted. 'Whose sword do you think this is?' She flashed the steely blade at him.

He looked at her, now understanding. 'I see. This was the reason you went down the well that night. This was your little secret.' His face softened. And with a slightly teasing ring to his voice he said, 'You do know how to use that don't you, girl? It's not a toy.'

His taunt only provoked her further and she violently pointed her sword at him. 'Out with your sword. Now!'

Vikraman raised his eyebrows. 'Really, you want to duel with me...Mekalai, you should know that I am unmatched in sword fighting.'

'Not in this town. Not yet,' she said impatiently.

He shrugged and unsheathed his sword.

She made the first move. He countered it. She deftly deflected his next attempt, moving gracefully in the air like a deer.

'Fight me like a man, Vikraman,' she breathed, crouching low. 'Don't patronize me just because I am a woman.'

In answer, he swung the blade at her and she had to duck. They duelled on ceaselessly, neither wanting to give up. Vikraman didn't want to hurt her and he had initially moved with caution but as time passed he was astounded by the dexterity of her moves. She was no novice, he realized.

He was playing a more defensive game than an offensive one, and as he warded off her steely blows, he couldn't but help admiring her even more; and her beauty dazzled him further. He saw how her curves moved in the air, he noted the tantalizing rise and fall of her breasts. Her hips swayed gracefully and her face was flushed with concentration. He wanted her now more than anything else.

Expertly fielding a forceful blow from her, he swung around to her side and caught her by the waist. She struggled in his arms, and holding her even more tightly, he said, 'Okay you win. Now you can claim your prize.'

And before she could respond, he crushed his lips against hers. She struggled against him, not wanting to give in. He could sense her resistance and it only aroused him further.

'Don't be silly, Mekalai,' he murmured, as his lips moved down her throat. 'You want this as much as I do. Your body cannot lie.'

He cupped her breasts and kneaded them, gently at first and then with increasing force. She gasped. He picked her up in his arms and carried her inside one of the hutments. He flung her onto the hay and pinned her down with his weight. He took one perfectly shaped bud into his mouth and she strained against him making whimpering noises. The urgency of his desire seared through her and she responded to his touch despite herself.

He planted love bites all the way down her neck and chest and she writhed in pleasure and pain. She pulsated with heat for him and he pressed down against her, cupping her buttocks. He wanted her desperately. He wanted her in the throes of passion like the other night, crying out to him, asking him not to stop. He parted her satiny thighs and she gasped in anticipation. He moved his tongue down there and she arched back wildly. Her fragrance, her sweet warmth engulfed him and he knew he had to have her now...

She pulled him up, her pupils dilating wildly with desire, and before he knew it, she had pinned him down on the hay and straddled him.

'Mekalai...' he groaned, seeing where she was going.

She planted hot, sweet kisses down his chest, driving him crazy. Then slowly, she eased herself down on him, crying out a little as he thrust up to meet her. She swayed erotically and he held her hips to keep her erect. They rocked together and in beautiful tandem. He moved into her as if they were part of each other and she threw her head back in pleasure as he moved up to enter into her deeper and deeper. Finally, they held each other, crying out one another's name. Poised on the brink of eternity consumed by their desire, they collapsed into each other's arms...

Nithilan returned to the hideout late in the night. First he and some other members of the band went to deposit the traitor, who was still bound to the tree, in a safe place where he wouldn't talk. When he returned he and Mekalai reunited in a joyful embrace, soon followed by tears. Nithilan took in his sister's persona, noting her love-struck eyes.

'I can see my sister has given her heart away,' he said gently, as he led her away to have a private talk.

She sighed deeply and said, 'Yes, irreversibly so. But I don't think he loves me.'

Nithilan shot her a sharp look. He had been given the impression that Vikraman too had intense feelings for her. Maybe he had been wrong. It was difficult to fathom what really went on in his leader's mind, and no one dared to ask. He paused, measuring his words carefully. 'He is an extraordinary man. It would be simple for any woman to fall for him. But he is a free spirit, not bound by the shackles of society.'

She looked up at her brother with troubled eyes. She said nothing and he didn't press the matter further either. But she got the gist of what he had said. It was what she herself believed.

That night as she lay under the star-sprinkled sky she was assailed by emotions she was unable to control. She felt uncontrollable elation whenever she thought of Vikraman. Her love made her happy and at the same time it filled her with infinite sadness. There was no proof that he loved her back. And she was too proud to ask him. Why should she beg him to love her? His desire and his passion, both were unmistakable. She had seen the look in his eyes. But love was a different animal. He wouldn't want to be bound by her. He had carved out a life for himself—an unusual life not for the faint of heart—and a woman would have no place in it. He is my first, but I am just one of the scores of women he must have had on his numerous adventures. The thought kept her awake almost until the uncertain pink of early dawn appeared over the horizon.

CHAPTER NINE

MEKALAI TASTED THE SALT in the air even as she and Vikraman sped along the coast on his black stallion the next night. The sun rose sleepily over the sky. Arikamedu was quite far and they wanted a head start. It was a little fishing village, known for its foreign connections. Vikraman had spent some time of his youth here but this he did not tell her just yet. She was dressed like a man, her long hair contained in a thick turban. She had wrapped a scarf around her face so no one would know she was a woman. And she had her sword. Her marvellous companion, her nightly comrade. Sheathed in its ornate, glistening cover, it hung from her slender waist.

The horse moved like the wind, his hooves almost a blur. Mekalai saw the twinkling lights of Poompuhar in the distance, even as they moved further away from it. She traced the outlines of the buildings, the graceful gopurams of the temples, and...Manikottai.

She saw it, diminishing in sight as they rode away, its sepulchral aura engulfing the air. She knew it was not over yet, this war between lust and love, between right and wrong, and ultimately, between good and evil. She knew she was at its epicentre, she was the catalyst. She also knew Narasimhan's fall would be by her hands. Poompuhar needed to erase this ominous black stain from its landscape, and it would soon happen.

Vikraman's men had brought tidings from the town, just before they had left. Narasimhan was like a rabid dog—murderous and furious. He couldn't believe that a mere bandit had managed to vanish with that slip of a girl into thin air. Where had he gone? And how had he entered the grounds in the first place? He had personally sacked each and every guard at Manikottai and appointed new ones. He had also dismissed his harem—perhaps his sexual hunger had vanished along with the girl. He could think of nothing else all night. He had put up a notice on the town square that anyone who knew anything about Mekalai's whereabouts was obliged to inform him.

But it was a futile exercise. Mekalai had vanished from the face of the earth, it seemed. No one knew where she was.

Mekalai knew that Narasimhan wouldn't rest until he had found her. That was why she had to find him first. She had said nothing of her resolution to Vikraman, knowing he would hear none of it; but this, she thought, was something she had to do.

The coastline seemed to fly by as Vikraman's stallion retained its pace. Mekalai felt the wind strongly, even against her covered face.

By the time they finally reached Arikamedu, Mekalai was drooping with exhaustion. They had ridden almost non-stop, pausing just once so the horse could get some rest and water. She slid off the horse wearily and let Vikraman prop her up with his arm.

It was still dark, even though the faint glow of dawn could be seen creeping up on the sky. They walked down a narrow lane, the horse's hooves making a clicking noise on the cobbled path.

At the end of that lane stood a house with three floors. It was surrounded by a lush garden on all sides. Vikraman took her inside. She walked through the gaily painted rooms generously decorated with plush ornate seats and beds, but was too overcome with fatigue to notice. She suddenly longed for the little thatched huts in the woods where she and Vikraman had lain entwined for hours. She had felt secure there.

Finally, they came to a little room and Vikraman ushered her in, urging her to go to sleep. She fell into a deep sleep and didn't wake till the sun was burning bright outside the window. Vikraman wasn't there and she wondered where he had disappeared. There was not a soul in the house and she wandered through its spacious, sunlit rooms with beautiful artefacts speckling the décor. She fingered some wine jars exquisitely crafted in glittery red glass, which she recognized for their Roman craftsmanship. She noted the porcelain urns and the marble busts. She took in the ostentatious silk rugs on the floor and the ivory chests. She opened one and saw that it was filled with exquisite, translucent, perfect pearls. They looked like little drops of dew against the dark blue velvet lining of the chest. She sank her fingers into them, letting their smooth texture graze against her skin.

Her gaze fell on the wall on her right. She walked towards it, enthralled. It held swords of every kind. Curved ones that could hook into a man's intestines in a second; sleek, snake-like ones; ornate ones; broad swords with their flared ends; swords for young princes, smaller in size with carvings of a hunting game engraved on them; tiny little daggers with looped handles meant for women to conceal in their garments.

Whose house was this? Who had collected these treasures so tastefully, so lovingly, in this strange, quiet house?

Lost in thought, she turned around to find Vikraman standing behind her.

'Where had you gone?' she asked, enveloping him in an embrace.

'Down to the port. I know some people there.'

'Whose house is this? It is beautiful.'

'Mine,' he said quietly. He smiled. It lit up her world.

'This is my house. It was the first sign I gave myself that I belonged to this world. That I had something to call my own. I lived here for many years, before I came to Poompuhar.'

A young boy appeared and nervously announced that

food was ready. As Mekalai followed, she once again reflected on how little she knew about the man she loved.

Rice cooked in rich ghee, fish cooked in a spicy, tangy gravy, steamed vegetables decorated with long tendrils of coconut, and roast meat awaited them. They ate out of silver plates and Mekalai noted that even the dining table had gold-plated legs.

'How...did you make so much money? She wanted to know.

'Pearl fishing,' came back the answer.

It made sense. Pearl fishing was the most lucrative business of the times. He had been a pearl fisher, possibly working only for himself, not for any king, merchant, or foreigner.

'I built all this in the last five years. It's not big but it's a place I love,' he said.

She understood his love for the house. It was like an old, wise soul. Its beauty was not harsh, it was peaceful.

They strolled around in the village. Little houses dotted the landscape along with the mandatory palatial mansions that towered over them. The opulence was unmistakable be it in their size or the sheer display of wealth.

They came to the bustling town square, and a beautiful temple that looked like it had just sprung from the earth, shone in the afternoon sun. Mekalai wandered around the market, stopping occasionally to try on the delicate tortoise shell bracelets, the colourful bead necklaces, and all other kinds of trinkets.

She kept a lookout for Vikraman but after a

while she lost him in the crowds. She saw a swish of exotic muslin, a hint of a shoulder perfect in its arch and fall. Vikraman was talking to this person but she couldn't see who it was except that it was a woman. She craned her neck to get a better view, but the crowds kept coming in the way, and by the time she had pushed her way through, the figure was gone and Vikraman was walking towards her.

'Whom were you talking to?' she asked, unable to keep the curiosity out of her voice.

'Just someone I knew from a long time ago,' said Vikraman lightly.

She did not ask him any further questions.

'There is to be a bullfight this evening. Here. I spoke to some people,' he said, his eyes shining with excitement.

'Are you going to participate?' she asked hesitantly. Bullfighting was a violent sport.

'Of course,' he answered. 'Mekalai, I live for this sort of thing. I thrive on danger.' She turned and walked away in anger.

'Mekalai, don't be vexed. I promise you no harm will come to me.'

She didn't say anything. Instead she gave him a long, hard look and walked away, back to the house, alone. But no amount of sulking or cold shouldering would make Vikraman change his mind. He had been doing this since he was fourteen, he said, and never once had he failed. She reluctantly agreed to go watch. But not before telling him what she thought.

'When I was six or seven, my father took me to a bullfight and I was horrified at how the bull dragged its opponent along the ground for a while, and then gored him with its horns. I have hated the sport ever since. I am not happy but you can do as you please,' she said, haughtily swinging her knee-length hair around. Vikraman suppressed a smile.

Whenever her friends would excitedly tell her about a bullfighting competition in Poompuhar, Mekalai would display scant enthusiasm.

'Men are truly foolish,' she would say, 'wanting to tame a raging bull. I have no time for such a brainless sport,' she would tell them firmly.

But they would have none of it. 'Don't you see, you featherbrain?' Lakshmi had squealed once. 'This is the perfect place to meet eligible young men. Brave, strong men who fear nothing in the world.' With that she had clapped her hands excitedly and proceeded to fuss over what she should wear in order to entice brave bullfighters.

The sky turned a deep scarlet that evening, almost as if it was aware of the bloody sport that was to take place under it. Bullfighting, or manju virattu was violent but rarely did the opponent kill the bull, unlike in some far-off exotic countries. It was not considered auspicious. Once the opponent had marked his victory over the animal, the animal would be drugged and dragged away. Nobody got seriously hurt unless things got out of control, but yes, a bullfighter needed to be prepared for injuries.

Judging by the long queue of participants, Mekalai calculated that it would be well past midnight before the sport would be over.

There was a buzz in the air and swarthy young men with strong, muscular arms, pumped by hours of exercise, roamed around. Vendors of liquor, sweetmeats, and other eatables were enjoying roaring business. The taverns nearby had filled up with customers who wanted to get some good toddy in their bellies before they proceeded to watch the blood and gore. Women with gleaming coffee-coloured skin moved around with sensuous grace, decked out in their finest. The prostitutes of Arikamedu stationed themselves at strategic points, waiting to lure potential customers who would soon retreat that way, tiring of watching the sport.

The arena was marked by a red rope that ran around the square. Flaming torches stood at all corners and could be used in the fight if needed. Barriers were set all around to protect the spectators. Mekalai wondered who would go in first.

The scent of blood was in the air. Vikraman stood there, towering over everybody else, his lean frame a sharp contrast to the hefty bodies of the other contestants. He had left his hair loose save for a scarf around his forehead, and the ringlets framed his face brilliantly, making him look like an utterly sensual demigod. His mouth was determined, and his eyes shone with the thrill of flirting with danger.

The bull was dragged in. It had a murderous air, the

whites of its eyes rolling madly. It snorted incessantly and moved its head from side to side violently. Its hooves scratched patterns on the sand as it circled the barriers, occasionally bumping into them, making the crowds squeal in excitement and terror.

Mekalai watched with a sort of horrific fascination as a slew of participants relented to their fight a little too easily. They were no match for the bull's rage. It seemed like a night when the beast would remain unvanquished until a tall, bronze-hued man with a thin bandage around his arm stepped up. Mekalai drew in her breath sharply. As angry as she was with him, she had no desire to see him hurt or wounded. But Vikraman exuded unabashed confidence. No other contestant had entered the arena with such an assured air. The bull too seemed to eye him testily. It snorted furiously at regular intervals and kept shifting on its feet, lunging forward occasionally. But Vikraman was ready for it. He circled the bull with mind-boggling agility. His movements were not rash and hurried like those of the other men. He measured his steps and it was like he could read the savage beast's mind. The bull was foaming at the mouth by now, perplexed by its opponent's wind-like movements.

Mekalai watched and clutched at her chest tightly. Her heart was threatening to explode with nervousness and she thought she was going to faint.

Then the mad dance began. The bull swayed violently and Vikraman kept moving around, waiting for an angle from which he could leap on its back in a final bid to tame it.

Vikraman was a blur even as he pounced on the beast's back. The bull lurched aggressively and Vikraman fell to the ground. The crowds roared. The bull swung forward and implanted its horns into him. Blood erupted from his shoulder and chest and Vikraman let out a primitive roar of pain. Mekalai screamed.

The bull hovered menacingly over its fallen opponent, preparing for its next attack. It happened at the speed of light. Despite his wounds, Vikraman's dexterity was unsurpassed. With a war cry, he swept himself from under the bull's head and in a split second, in which time seemed to stand still for Mekalai, he hoisted himself on to the bull's back and grabbed its horns. The crowds went berserk. The bull convulsed in anger and panic for a few seconds and then seemed to calm down. Volunteers rushed to tie it up and just as they entered the arena, Vikraman collapsed on to the ground, unconscious. But just before he lost conciousness, he saw a visage above his head. His last thought before he passed out was that he had died and gone to heaven and an angel was hovering over him.

Mekalai never fully remembered the details of how she had managed to get Vikraman back to the house. She remembered arms, a lot of dismembered arms—she couldn't recall the bodies they were attached to—rushing to hold up Vikraman. His shoulder spurting blood, they heaved him out of the chaos and set him down on the ground. Mekalai ran to him, shaking with fear. She quickly tore off a long piece of her upper robes and tightly bandaged his shoulder so the flow of blood would stop.

'Stop...please stop...' she beseeched the wound. The blood stained her robe, emitting its steely odour. Vikraman half sat up.

She propped him up on her shoulder and somehow, with surprising strength, managed to heave him up. She again recalled that hands and shoulders had appeared, along with concerned voices; and with their help, she got him back to the house.

Mekalai flung open the doors of the house, all the while supporting Vikraman's frame. Her helpers had departed after depositing him inside the house.

Thankfully, the young boy employed there scrambled into action and with his help, she quickly took Vikraman to one of the rooms and laid him on the bed. Mekalai rushed to prepare a lepam of medicinal herbs and leaves, while the young boy sat beside Vikraman. She came back into the room carrying the paste in a silver cup and unflinchingly applied it to the wounds.

The agony seemed endless. By midnight, a raging fever had broken out and a tearful Mekalai had sent the young boy out to look for a physician. The boy returned with a very old bent man whose straggly beard touched the ground. His rheumy eyes held infinite wisdom and Mekalai at once felt she could trust him.

He walked into Vikraman's room and shut the door for what seemed like centuries to Mekalai.

Finally when he emerged, he had a look of satisfaction on his face. 'The bull's horns had been plated with copper, which is not uncommon in these parts,' he said. 'The edges were unusually sharp and that deepened the wound. I have applied my herbal paste on it and he should be fine within a couple of days.'

His sage eyes regarded Mekalai. He saw a beautiful, troubled face brimming over with love. 'He is a brave man,' he said quietly. 'You should have nothing to worry about.'

Then the wait began. Vikraman's fever broke and then returned. Even though the physician had told her it would happen, she panicked. He muttered her name in his delirium and mumbled other things she couldn't fathom. He tossed and turned, and once he opened his eyes to find the same angel above his head and he wondered if he had died and gone to heaven. The face floated around his head, it seemed in his semi-conscious state. Mekalai bathed the wounds regularly, reapplying the strong-smelling murky green paste the physician had given her. She dabbed his scorching body with a cool cloth and didn't move from his side. Finally after four full days, Vikraman stirred. He called out her name weakly. She rushed to his side, relief flooding her heart. He sat up with her help, his face looking weak with exhaustion and fever.

She called out to the young boy to bring some watery rice gruel and when it came, Vikraman gulped it down hungrily. His hunger appeased, he slumped back on the bed and his eyes closed. She left the room.

The sun had beat a hasty retreat that day, ushering in a silvery twilight. Night fell and Mekalai, unable to stay within the walls of the house any more, stepped out to inhale the flower-scented night air.

Palmyra dotted the edges of the orchard and the intoxicating fragrance of her favourite flower the frangipani, rose in the air. She plucked a champakam from a low-hanging branch and tucked it behind her ear. A minstrel's voice floated in, his plaintive chords weaving a soothing love song. There was passion in it and sacrifice, and unending love. He spoke of lovers who had gone away, never to return; and he spoke of the hearts of young girls, broken to smithereens by heartless strangers from exotic lands. He sang of unrequited love, and plucking on his little stringed instrument he wandered along, unaware of the effect he had had on the young girl who stood shimmering like a mirage in the moon-soaked garden.

Come find me, O song of the night,

Let me place your melody on my lips...

My soul wanders over the seven seas, in search of you

Come find me, O song of the night...

The minstrel paused by the massive, carved entrance and blinked at the vision in front of him. His lyrical heart recognized her. The poets of Thanjavur hadn't been wrong. They sang odes to her beauty, her striking beauty, and he found their verses etched on herself.

He smiled. 'The poets knew what they were talking about.'

She couldn't fathom what he was saying. 'If I were younger, I would write a fresh ode to your purity, your spirit. I see it,' he said, this minstrel with eyes that seemed to belong to a very far-off time.

She felt an inexplicable connection with this wizened old man whose face seemed haunted by life. When he asked her for a drink of water she ushered him inside. He stood outside on the porch and took a full deep swig. When she asked him if he wanted anything stronger, he chuckled. She asked the boy to bring him some of the exotic liquor that was stored in the teakwood cupboard in the kitchen.

As he nursed the golden goblet in his gnarled hands, the minstrel began to hum another song.

Oh, tell me where I can find her
The goddess whose beauty courses through my soul
She scorches my heart with her blazing smile
And I shrivel, burn, and turn to ashes...

She sat on the cool steps, her hands cupping her chin as she listened him. His song soothed her soul, her troubled heart.

'Were you always a wandering minstrel? Where is your home?' she asked.

He laughed soundlessly, revealing a mouth with a number of missing teeth.

'The earth is my home and the wind is my carriage. But yes, long ago my home was in your town, your beautiful land of abundance. But I have left for good. I will never go there again,' he said, his watery eyes spilling over.

She wanted to ask him why but something told her to remain quiet.

'I have secrets, my child, dark ghosts from the past that haunt me...' He tipped the goblet into his mouth and continued.

'I don't know why I am telling you all this. I haven't spoken about it in ages but something about you makes me want to tell you...'

The liquor had him in its hold as his tongue loosened.

'I was happy. I served a master who was good and kind. A master who wanted to believe the best of everyone. He gave people third and fourth chances and invariably they let him down. I was his valet, the only man who had access into his inner chamber. He trusted me with his life and I was unable to save it.'

He wiped away his helpless tears.

'My mistress was good and kind too. She was a perfect match for her husband. She had a pure soul, a gentle voice. But she was not my master's first wife. His first wife was a woman who only held darkness in her heart. It crept up to her eyes too. I have dreams about it even today. And her son, I swear he was the spawn of the devil if there exists one. Even as a child, he loved to hurt those weaker than him. I have seen him wring the neck of his pet parrot in rage. I have seen him stone little puppies to death. His mother took devilish pleasure in her son's antics and encouraged him. By the time he was twenty, he was a living monument of everything dark and evil. The king loved his younger son. He was like his mother. He was bright, he was good, and he displayed all the qualities one needed to be a leader. My master decided that his younger son would inherit his wealth and power. He planned to alter his will as soon as he could. He told the evil son as much. That was his big mistake. When the older one got to know he plotted a hellish conspiracy. He crept into my master's chamber at night and wrung his neck with his bare hands. His own father. He left him there to die, and when I found him, the last breath had escaped from his being. His eyes were still alive and I could see the pools of tragedy in them.'

Mekalai listened to this story that she had heard before in total silence. A tide washed over her mind and she furiously fought against it, wanting him to complete the story.

'I ran, ran to save my sweet mistress and her son. I didn't want to see their blood spilled too. But I was too late. I ran into her chamber only to see the young master bent over his mother's crumpled corpse. Blood stained the floor and ran in rivulets. She must have struggled. And he knifed her.

'I picked up the young master and ran. But there he was standing at the doorway, a tower of doom. He caught the young boy the way one holds a lamb to be slaughtered, and drew out his knife and aimed it at him, when the boy kicked. The knife hit his arm and carved out a deep winding wound. I still remember the way blood sprang up and made its little path along the gash.

'My little master ran, he could run like the wind. He ran past the confused guards and past the sentinels at the main gate. He pushed open the gates and then was gone forever. I don't know if he is alive or dead. And I am too old to do anything about it.'

She stared into the man's face but she was not really looking at it. She was gazing into the endless sea of time. She saw the story come alive before her eyes, she smelt the blood, the fear; she felt the unfathomable sorrow. Threads unravelled and pieces fell into place. The wind whistled around as if waiting to hear what happened next.

Mekalai finally asked the question she had been meaning to ask since the beginning of the minstrel's narration.

'What was the boy's name?' she asked, despite knowing the answer already.

The old man buried his face in his hands and groaned. He told her the name.

It seemed like aeons until she could move. She slowly got up and left the porch, leaving the old man sobbing. As she went into the house, she could hear him leaving and soon she heard the faint strains of his voice streaming through the wind.

Sadness is a sea, I drown in it...
Carry me O wind, carry me far away
Let the moonlight soothe me with its caress...

Vikraman saw her framed against the doorway. She had a wispy quality to her and in his weak state he was convinced she was an illusion—that none of this was real. A celestial being had descended on earth to take his heart and soul and now she would disappear into spirals of thin white light.

Mekalai walked into the room slowly. She sat by the bed and looked at him.

'That's how you knew...that's how you knew the secret doorway was there. You always knew it.'

He was too startled to react.

'You know every inch of Manikottai, don't you? You have travelled through every passage, every staircase. You have looked into those mirrors, you have slept in those beds. Only, when you lived there, it was a haven of happiness and peace, not the hell it has become today.'

His face displayed emotions of every kind. She took his arm and traced his scar with her forefinger. She bent down and kissed the knitted lines of skin.

'I wanted to tell you,' he said emotionally. 'I wanted to tell you everything. But I just didn't want to put you in further danger. If you knew my connection to Manikottai, it would only make you more vulnerable to my enemy.'

He held her face in his hands and drew her into a long, loving kiss. She was engulfed in it, the sea of his sadness, the depths of his love.

He then told her his story. He had fled from the fortress and a group of fishermen stowed him in their Korkai-bound catamaran. He spent the night under a few stinking sacks, shivering in the cold, with the wind howling around him. The next day, the fishermen had given him some silver coins and left him to his devices in Korkai. He wandered around for days with no proper food or shelter. He stayed away from the palace guards or any other officials because he didn't want the news carried to Manikottai. Eventually a pearl merchant took him under his wing and taught him the trade. He sat in the shop watching sacks and sacks of the luminous little orbs being brought in, and he was fascinated. He was in awe of the Greeks and the Romans, with their thick curls and golden skin and the way they manipulated the business to their advantage. Soon he learnt to dive for pearls. He loved sinking to the bottom of the seabed and closing his hands around the gleaming oysters. He loved the deep blues and greens, the animated life deep under water. Soon he was diving for his own pearls and he sold them in the market. He gave the foreign traders a good deal and they learnt to trust the young good-looking boy with bright, keen, honest eyes.

'Eventually I moved to Arikamedu. I loved the village and its untouched quality. I built myself a house here.'

But the nightmare of Manikottai never left him. He relived the horror every night, waking up in clammy spasms, drenched with sweat, and finally he decided that his parents' death had to be avenged.

'I wanted to walk into Manikottai and kill Narasimhan with my bare hands. But I knew I wouldn't stand a chance against him. I needed to be patient and clever,' he recalled.

Tales of Narasimhan's tyranny continued to reach him and one day when he was about twenty, he single-handedly stopped a cart carrying an illegal shipment of precious gems on their way to the coffers of Manikottai. It had actually been easy. Armed with just a spear, he had barred the way on a dusty mud track, and the two guards accompanying the loot had wet their dhotis at the sight of the tall, masked man with a blazing fire in his eyes. He had rejoiced when he heard that Narasimhan had been livid with rage at the news. He had also distributed the gems among the poor.

From then on it was easy. A certain fear came to be attached to his name and he was soon known, revered, and feared as the masked thief of Poompuhar. He had collected a small but strong following during his travels and adventures. And he came back to Poompuhar and set up base at its deepest core—the woods.

'Now the time has come,' he said, 'to see this bloody saga to its denouement. With you involved, I have to end it. Now it is him and me and nothing else.'

She listened in silence. All her life she had wished for drama, for adventure, and now when she had it, she wondered if it was really worth it. 'Nothing is worth the life of the man you love,' she thought.

Defeating Narasimhan would not be an easy task. He had might and power. But if there was anyone who could do it, she was certain it was Vikraman.

Vikraman's lips sought hers and they melted into each other, savouring each second, making it last, as if this was the only night they would ever be together again. They spent the night in each other's arms.

Vikraman's recovery was slow but steady. He was still weak and needed help to walk around, but the wound was healing fast. Now that Mekalai knew everything, Vikraman wanted to go back to Poompuhar at the earliest. He saw no point in further delay. He wanted to seize the moment and strike.

But the physician had other plans for him. 'Your body needs rest, young man,' he had admonished severely. 'Whatever your grand plans may be, they can wait.' And Vikraman slumped back on to his cushions, disheartened.

A few nights later, Mekalai had just stepped out of Vikraman's room when she realized that there was someone waiting in the main hall.

It was the woman's body language that first held Mekalai. It had a supremely erotic quality to it. She then turned to Mekalai who suddenly felt awkward and heavy-limbed in comparison to the grace with which the other woman moved. The woman was dressed in diaphanous robes that seemed like liquid against her dusky gleaming skin. Her eyes glittered and her lips were painted a deep, inviting red. She was not young, but age had only enhanced her appeal. She was intoxicating, like old wine. She walked towards Mekalai, a deeply mysterious smile on her face. She took in the girl's compelling beauty, not yet ravaged by time.

Then she spoke. Her words floated out of her mouth in low musical tones. Mekalai wondered if she had managed to install a nightingale in her throat—no human voice could be that captivating. And with a start, Mekalai realized where she had heard this voice before. It was in the marketplace, the day before the bullfight. She remembered a swirl of robes and an exotic fragrance, and she knew she had heard these same dulcet tones addressing Vikraman.

'Where is he?' the woman asked.

Mekalai was unable to answer so she gestured towards the room in which Vikraman lay fast asleep.

The woman floated sensuously across the room, past Mekalai, and looked into the other room.

'He is asleep. I will not wake him,' she purred. 'I was away when this unfortunate accident took place. Vikraman always did like to provoke danger. Is he better now?'

Mekalai nodded.

'Do you have a voice you can use or has Vikraman found himself a bird that cannot sing?' the woman asked sweetly.

Mekalai's eyes flashed. 'Well, that depends. This *bird* does not sing for everyone.'

The woman laughed. It made a tinkling noise.

'I am Tilottama. I have known Vikraman for a long time...intimately...'

She said the last word with an erotic swirl. Mekalai was seriously disconcerted but she covered up with a haughty smile.

'Whatever that means really.'

'Well, my dear child, it means exactly what it does in your parts of the world as in mine.'

She showed off her perfect white teeth, her lips curved in a teasing smile.

'Hasn't he told you yet, little mite...has he never mentioned me?'

'No,' said Mekalai, still maintaining her haughty stance.

Tilottama paced the room like a cat on the prowl—soft, diabolic, and feline.

'Vikraman has a way with women...I taught him that way,' she said smugly. 'I am sure he has impressed his superior carnal knowledge on you, more than once, and I would like to take full credit for it.'

Mekalai listened, jealousy mounting like an ugly, slimy green monster in her head. How dare this woman just walk in and start talking about Vikraman's sexual escapades? How dare she refer to him in that tone?

She suddenly realized that Tilottama was watching her keenly. She rearranged her expression to one of extreme haughtiness once again. Losing control over her emotions would only add to this vile woman's glee. She had to act grown up, she had to keep her composure against all odds.

Tilottama walked around the room, looking lazily at the curios. Finally she came to the ivory chest, the one that Mekalai loved so much. She stroked it with her fingers the same way Mekalai had done, but when she did it, the action was steeped in sensuality.

'I was the first woman Vikraman ever had. I set the benchmark for his women. He likes them experienced, not simpering virgins.'

Mekalai said nothing, refusing to respond to the taunt.

'I met him here in Arikamedu. Our eyes met across the town square, I remember. He came looking for me that night...'

Her voice trailed off.

'He used to read poetry to me, he painted me in the nude. He would come to the brothel and not leave for days. We would stay in my room locked up...'

'Why are you telling me all this,' asked Mekalai, finally cutting the woman short.

'I am telling you because you are a foolish young girl who has unfortunately given her heart away to an uncharted storm. Vikraman is a free spirit. He will not be contained. Any girl who tries to keep him has lost him. Ask me.'

Mekalai listened, rooted to the spot.

'But he has a stronger bond with me than he

will ever admit to himself. He moved from Korkai, where his business was based, to be with me here in Arikamedu. He built a home here. And today when he needs shelter he returns here, to the town in which I live.'

Her scent was beginning to make Mekalai sick. She wished the woman would leave. Go away forever and take this bitter truth she had brought in back with her.

Tilottama came closer to Mekalai. 'Vikraman is wild, untamed...like me. I let him go, so he comes back to me...as he will at the end of it all.'

By now Mekalai's fury was beginning to rise to its full tide. Her bosom heaving in agitation, she almost screamed, 'Get out, get out of this house!'

Tilottama turned to go, but not without a backward glance. 'Better to be safe than sorry, my darling. It's cruel to have your heart permanently dashed to smithereens at such a young age...'

With that she walked out, leaving behind traces of her exotic, musky fragrance and words that had caused immeasurable pain.

Mekalai sank down on to the soft Persian carpet. Tilottama had said nothing that she didn't know already, she reflected. Vikraman didn't love her. He was intrigued by her beauty. He desired her carnally. And she would have to be content with that.

Tears fell copiously and then she shook herself. 'You are made of sterner stuff than this,' she told herself firmly. She made up her mind. She would be with Vikraman till he had vanquished Narasimhan. She was linked to that destiny. But beyond that, her future was hers, hers alone to contemplate. She would let Vikraman go.

Over the next few days, a dark cloud descended upon Mekalai's mood. Vikraman noticed it, but he put it down to worry and exhaustion. His concerned eyes watched her, but she also seemed distant all of a sudden. He let her be, his heart breaking in the process. He longed to touch her, hold her in his arms, and kiss her passionately, but he refrained. Her silence was mystifying, but something about her stance told him not to broach the topic. 'It will all work out in the end,' he told himself.

One night, he left the house and didn't return until morning. Mekalai had lain in bed, tormented by the thought that he had gone to visit Tilottama. She pictured them in bed together, their bodies writhing in ecstasy, and she couldn't bear it. When he returned, he offered no explanation, only telling her that they should leave for the forest the next day. She hardly responded and even when he tried to draw her close, she pulled away, muttering some pretext.

Mekalai was sorry to leave the house in Arikamedu. She had fallen in love with its quiet beauty and wished she could linger there. Vikraman had news from Nithilan, who thought that Narasimhan had given up the search for his fugitive runaway bride. He had focused all his frustrated energies on capturing the smaller provinces sprinkled around Poompuhar, relieving various overlords and chieftains of their responsibilities. After one particularly bloody victory, he marched through the gates of Poompuhar, his army in tow, with the head of the chief in his hand.

This had put him in a good mood and he had ordered celebrations to be held. The most exotic dancers were brought in for him from all over, and for two days, the chieftain revelled in a maze of liquor, women, and euphoria.

It was safe to return to the woods now, Nithilan said in his letter, but he advised that neither Vikraman nor Mekalai set foot in Poompuhar. Not yet.

Clutching the ornate gold dagger as a keepsake, Mekalai mounted the stallion along with Vikraman. They sped back along the route they had come, in the dead of the night. He could feel her body pressing against his, the thin muslin clinging to her curves, and it surged through him once again how much he loved her and wanted her.

The town square was bustling with excitement. Narasimhan had proclaimed that celebrations be held and preparations were on. Huge pandals were erected, large vilakkus with their graceful peacock mouths stood at every corner. Nautch girls roamed around the square in their sensuous best. A colossal, exquisitely carved gold throne was put on the dais at the main pandal. A wrestling match was to be held—

Narasimhan's favourite sport after womanizing. And this wrestling match was the opportunity Vikraman was waiting for.

'I am going to participate. This way I can get closer to him. Tonight is the night, Mekalai.'

'No! 'she protested. 'There must be other ways of vanquishing this demon. This is too dangerous. It's too open,' she said stifling a sob before he could see it.

He regarded her solemnly. 'This is the only way. He has doubled the guards at Manikottai and fortified it even more. The secret passage has been blocked. Going into Manikottai to challenge him would be nothing but foolhardy.'

'I want to be there too,' she cried. 'I would drive myself mad if I was here and didn't know what was happening out there.' But he would hear none of it.

'For once restrain yourself, Mekalai,' he said a little roughly. 'You have to stay here.'

She nodded, not arguing further. She prayed to Goddess Durga for strength and gripped her own sword with steely grit. She would be there, to shield him, to protect him.

Nithilan and other members of the band set out at various times for the town square. Some were heavily disguised and others, who still led double lives, went as themselves. Mekalai waited till Vikraman sped away. She had looked wide-eyed and innocent while saying goodbye, and he had regarded her a little suspiciously.

'You are not up to anything, are you? You look too innocent for your own good today.'

‘Of course not,’ she said demurely. ‘I shall sit here by the fire and wait for your return.’

His look of suspicion darkened but he said nothing. After engulfing her in a crushing embrace and planting a kiss on her brow, he sped away.

Mekalai watched him go, her heart heavy.

Wrestlers entered the town square arena, gleaming with oil, their minuscule komanams hanging precariously from their posterior. Vikraman was one of them. He had covered his face with a scarf like many of them had, and he passed easily through the barricades. Mekalai crept into the crowd quietly. She had covered her face well and had removed all her expensive jewellery so as to not attract attention.

A koothu was on to kick off the evening, and the dancers moved rhythmically to the beat of the musical instruments. The din sounded hollow and boomed in the air and it subsided only when Narasimhan walked on to the dais. The dancers exited.

Narasimhan looked ominously larger than life. His gigantic frame loomed large over everything. His thick arms were the size of young palm trees and his chest looked wide enough to house a residential colony. He was dressed in a quilted coat of black and gold and his robes had diamonds and rubies sewn on it. Once again Mekalai reflected that if Yama had a human form it would probably be this. He raised his massive arms and the crowds’ murmur faded out.

‘Let the competition begin,’ he announced in his booming voice. Trumpets blared over the town square.

The participants paired off. The last man standing would then wrestle with Narasimhan's own prize wrestler, and it was this violent match that he actually looked forward to. His wrestler had a penchant for tearing people apart with his bare hands.

Mud flew in the air as the competitors began to fight. This was a brutal game. There were no rules and only strength, cunning, and prowess counted. More than strength and prowess, cunning was crucial, Vikraman reflected. He had lingered back in the queue, wanting to go last. He knew he would easily be able to defeat his opponent but what he really wanted was a chance to go up on the dais on the pretext of challenging the court wrestler.

Finally his turn came. His opponent had defeated four of his predecessors and looked pumped up with victory. Vikraman's agility won him the first round of gauging and attacking. His opponent was far stronger and bigger built than him and he knew that only guile could get him past his competitor. Out of the corner of his eye he saw Narasimhan watch the contest keenly. He was interested in the youth—his grace and dexterity was remarkable. He watched his cat-like moves, never repeating the same pattern again, keeping his assailant guessing. The crowds rippled in tension. Mekalai couldn't breathe out of her rising panic. She knew Nithilan was there somewhere in the crowd but she had no way of knowing where. Another deft move from Vikraman countered a potential attack, and the crowds screamed for more. Mekalai had her heart in her mouth.

Finally in a blurry, agile move, Vikraman landed a kick on the man's exposed ribcage and he fell to the ground with a pained shout.

In the midst of the thunderous roar of the people, Vikraman ascended the steps to the dais. Mekalai inched closer to the barriers separating the dais from the throngs, her heart fluttering like a pigeon's wings.

The feudal chieftain took in the young man who was steadily, confidently approaching him. He looked familiar. Narasimhan thought back, trying to sift through his rapier-sharp memory and figure out where he could have encountered this man before, but he couldn't place him. He looked into those clear, keen eyes and something stirred within him. It unsettled him, took him to places he had long buried in the deep recesses of his memory. He took in the man's frame and noticed the thin muslin bandage around his right arm. His gaze lingered there for a while. By now Vikraman had reached the centre of the dais.

Narasimhan raised his eyebrows and then said, 'Well, my young man, you fought rather well. I am impressed. Now let's see how you tackle Vallavan here. If you succeed in overthrowing him, a thousand gold ingots are yours for the taking.'

Mekalai had by now reached the front of the barricade. Pressing her slender frame against the iron fences, she watched. Vikraman did not even spare Vallavan a glance.

'I am not interested in the prize money. Donate it to the temple. And as for him, I'm sure I can defeat him easily,' said Vikraman, projecting a touch of arrogance. 'I think you know that too, sir.'

Narasimhan let out a deafening laugh. 'How can you be so sure, young man? And if you are so confident, why not let your actions speak louder than these arrogant words?'

'I will fight him. On one condition.'

'What is it?' asked Narasimhan impatiently. But his curiosity got the better of him and he rearranged his features to a slightly more amiable expression.

'If I defeat this Ghatotkach here,' he said, waving a nonchalant hand at the troll-like wrestler, 'I want to have the honour of fighting you.'

The crowds murmured in horror, shaking their heads.

Narasimhan looked like he might explode, but managed to control himself.

'Don't you think you are going too far, young man? First you refuse my prize money, then you insult my prize wrestler, and now you want to fight me?' He jeered and his courtiers sniggered courteously.

Vikraman looked unperturbed as he responded. 'I am aware that my desire is, well, a little off limits, but at the risk of sounding totally impudent, I know you are intrigued.' Narasimhan fixed a sharp eye on his face as he considered how to react. Vikraman could almost hear the wheels turning in the tyrant's head as he battled between his pride and his curiosity.

Finally Narasimhan drew in a deep breath and said, 'So be it.'

Vallavan flexed his muscles. He stepped into the dusty arena and each step the giant took made the dust fly in all directions. Vikraman studied his adversary as they circled each other. Vallavan was making low, grunting noises and Vikraman could sense that he was in some discomfort. He took note of his opponent's length and saw that he was dragging his left foot a little, from which he deduced an injury. That was where he should aim, he thought. Vallavan aimed a sharp blow and it caught Vikraman on the chin. He staggered back but kept his balance. Vikraman got on all fours and sprinted like a tiger across the arena. In a blinding flash, he aimed a blow at Vallavan's foot and the seven foot-tall wrestler toppled over, letting out a deafening roar before falling to the ground, unconscious.

There was a total hush in the audience as they all turned their eyes towards Narasimhan. Mekalai watched, her heart pounding. The tyrant slowly rose from his throne and walked down to the arena.

'Who are you?' He directed the question more like an imperial command.

Vikraman smiled. It wasn't a pleasant smile. It brought a shiver even to the cold-blooded chieftain's heart.

'Ghosts of the past can return to haunt you, Narasimhan,' he said with a dangerous quietude in his voice.

'Think hard, run your vile mind through all

the unpardonable sins you have committed in your lifetime. Recall the scars you etched on innumerable lives.' Narasimhan stared at Vikraman, comprehension dawning on his face.

'You...' he said under his breath.

'Yes, me,' said Vikraman. He lifted up his arm and slowly peeled off the muslin bandage to reveal the deep, winding scar. Narasimhan gazed at it for some time and then lifted his eyes to meet Vikraman's blazing ones.

And then he let out a sarcastic laugh.

'So now what? What are you going to do? Kill me?' he jeered. He thumped his chest and roared. 'This slip of a man wants to kill me.' His laughter boomed across the town square.

Vikraman's eyes blazed with fury. 'I have waited years to avenge the death of my parents. I knew you thought me to be dead but luckily, I survived. For once you failed to take someone's life, Narasimhan, and today it's your turn.'

'You can never hope to defeat me. I am too strong,' said Narasimhan.

'Let's leave that to fate, shall we?' said Vikraman quietly.

Narasimhan stepped down from the dais. Two attendants scrambled behind him to relieve him of his black-and-gold quilted coat. Beneath the quilted coat, he was wearing a gleaming waistband with a steely glint. Vikraman remained where he was. Narasimhan walked up to him and when they were just a few paces from each other, he said sneeringly, 'Bow to your death, Vikraman. You will soon be united with our honourable father, and your mother, pathetic, frail creature.'

He spat the last words out and Vikraman could contain himself no longer. He lunged forward aiming a blow, which Narasimhan countered almost effortlessly. His strength was legendary. Vikraman reeled back violently from the impact. He recovered quickly and in a lightning-quick move, he planted a kick on Narasimhan's granite-hard chest. It sent the tyrant flying. Dust rose up like a storm. Narasimhan slowly picked himself up and took a deep breath. The crowds watched in horrific fascination as the two circled each other like kites in the sky. There was a compelling animal quality to them and everyone was riveted despite their bewilderment and confusion.

Mekalai swiftly moved around to the side nearest to them. She had to do something, she thought frantically. She had to help Vikraman. She had irreversibly given her heart to him and she would love him forever. She watched the two men—one much taller and mightier than the other, who was swift, supple, and light-footed, like a tiger.

Vikraman's mind was racing. He knew he would never win this war by matching Narasimhan strength to strength. He needed something else.

'Know something else, Narasimhan,' he said between clenched teeth, in a low tone that only his enemy could hear. 'I was the one that night, who took your bride away from you. I am the masked thief of Poompuhar, the bandit you so loathe. What will you do *now?*'

The taunting words had their desired effect. Narasimhan's eyes held a mad rage. Vikraman could see the whites of his bloodshot eyes alive with absolute fury. The lessons he had learnt from various masters over the years came to Vikraman's mind. He thought of the Chinese trader who had been a sniper in his king's army, who had taught him some invaluable tricks. Tricks...he closed his eyes...

What happened next was barely visible to the onlookers as it happened so fast. The sharp, stylish blow landed on Narasimhan's neck. The crowd's roar rose in tidal waves. Narasimhan landed on the ground, spreadeagled. Vikraman bent over his motionless body without any expression on his face. He rose and scanned the stunned crowd. He saw the eyes he had painted, kissed, loved. He saw the face, divine, unforgettable, with rivulets of tears running down its cheeks, he saw the woman he had loved since the beginning of time...

There was a slight movement behind him. Unheeding, he walked towards the barricade. As he approached her, he heard a rustle at the back. He swung around, comprehending in a flash, but Narasimhan was too quick for him.

Vikraman swerved as the dagger came at him, and instead of hitting his chest, it hit his shoulder, reopening the still raw bullfighting wound. Blood trickled in little streams down his shoulders. Narasimhan struck again, his face contorted and disfigured by wrath and vehemence. As his hand came down, the dagger poised for a second stab, his expression changed.

Surprise reigned supreme on Narasimhan's visage as he felt the swift, steely penetration in his stomach. The colour drained from Narasimhan's face as he buckled and collapsed on his knees, Mekalai's searing persona reflected in his eyes. In her face, he saw Durga. She held a gem-encrusted sword in her hand, its tip stained with crimson. She looked like a goddess scorned, her dark tresses whipping around her like a storm and her scorching eyes flickering with the pulse of anger.

Blood spurted out of him, as if in a hurry to leave his body. He looked at Mekalai one last time and then crumpled into a massive heap on the ground. Narasimhan was dead.

CHAPTER TEN

CHAOS ENSUED ALL AROUND. Narasimhan's guards went scattering all over the place not knowing what to do or whose orders to follow. The crowd was agog with excitement, horror, and confusion. A girl drove a sword into Narasimhan's gut and he was no longer alive to torment them, abduct their women, and seize their land! The people of Poompuhar danced with joy.

Vikraman reeled around frantically to capture the face of the woman who had saved his life. This beautiful, extraordinary, brave woman. Passion and love surged through his being. But she was gone in a flash. In all the pandemonium, she had evaporated like a cloud. Many had recognized her, the divine beauty who had captivated everyone in their town, and they were all astounded.

'It was Mekalai,' they kept saying, over and over again.

Vikraman was surrounded by throngs of people who wanted to reach out and touch him, the valiant hero who had challenged their despotic ruler. The people of Poompuhar had finally received a saviour. Tearing a piece of cloth from his scarf and tying it hastily over his wound, he pushed past them, weaving his way through the multitudes to catch up with Mekalai. He was perplexed by her behaviour.

She shimmered in the distance like a mirage and then she was gone.

Mekalai kept walking. She didn't know where she was going. She passed the town square, riotous with celebrations over a tyrant's assassination. She passed the colourful markets, oblivious to the wares on display. She walked though the open fields, not noticing the flowers in bloom. She ignored the little children on the street, playing with their bows and arrows and their mock swords. Everything was a blur as she stormed past, wanting to get away from everything, most of all herself.

She had carried the sword today knowing deep inside that she would use it. Use it against an evil force that had threatened to trample her world under his vicious power. But with his end came the end of her association with Vikraman. He would be free of her now, free to go to the woman he really wanted to be with, free to love anyone without being bound by a foolish young girl who had acted impetuously and let herself be led by her heart.

She turned the corner that led to the river bank. The sun had begun its fiery descent into the waters. She sat by the grassy bank, watching the orange orb dip into the sea languorously. Not long ago, a young man had stopped her here suggesting that she was haunting him. It was ironical that the opposite was true. She sighed wearily. She would return to her home, now that it was all over. Nithilan was now free to come back home and live with her. 'I suppose I may have to marry some rich merchant from Madurai just to keep him happy. He will not want to see his sister unwed,' she told herself.

There was a hollow gnawing in her heart. A vacuum she felt would never be filled. She heard footsteps behind her and she turned. She looked up to see the face she loved so much. A face that gazed down at her, confusion etched deep on its beautiful features. She rose. Vikraman said nothing but continued to gaze at her. His eyes seemed to bore into her, she felt a warmth course through her blood. Her senses tingled.

'You forgot your sword in your hurry to run away from me,' he said quietly, handing over the gleaming blade to her. She took it, not meeting his eyes. His gaze seemed to ask a thousand questions. He looked serious and dangerously calm as he addressed her. 'Why did you run away, Mekalai?' he asked. 'Why did you run away? You saved my life. You are an incredible, extraordinary woman but I don't understand you at all.'

She didn't meet his eyes. She could feel the tears pricking her eyelids as she spoke. 'I...I wanted to get away. Now that all this is over, you can be free of me...' Tears flowed down her cheeks.

Bewilderment and shock rippled through his face.

'What are you talking about, you foolish girl? Rid of you, how can I ever be rid of you,' he cried hoarsely. 'I love you Mekalai. I want you in this life and in every other life I might have...'

The words sounded like a sweet melody to her ears, but she still couldn't believe him. He had always held back, never giving her any answers. And he had never told her until now that he desired her completely, not just her body.

'What has come over you? Why do you have such doubts?' he asked, holding her roughly.

'She told me,' Mekalai cried. '*She*, the love of your life. She told me that you would go back to her ultimately, no matter where you wandered...' she trailed off tearfully. The look of disbelief on his face was enough to make her feel foolish and small. Vikraman cupped her face in his hands. His eyes seemed to bore into the depths of her soul.

'She is lying, Mekalai. She is just jealous of you. She has been in love with me for too long now and I don't reciprocate her feelings. She may have meant something to me at some point in my life, but never have I felt for any woman what I feel for you. I don't love her. I love you. I love you, my darling,' he said, his voice thick with emotion.

'But then two nights later, you disappeared and I assumed you were with her...you never gave me an explanation...' she continued between gulps and sobs.

He clicked his tongue in exasperation. 'I went out

to gather information. I didn't think you would make a mountain out of a molehill over it in your mind.'

The sun had set, leaving a hazy purple glow over the world. Vikraman looked at Mekalai. She looked like a rose in full bloom. A melody waiting to be sung. He drew her closer to him and said, overcome with emotion, 'Be mine, Mekalai, be mine forever. Marry me and bear me my children—extraordinary, brave, beautiful children, just like their mother. Marry me. I want to stand here by the banks of the Kaveri with you even when I am eighty years old. The Kaveri that has been a witness to our love from the start...'

She rested her head against his chest, letting the warmth of his strong arms engulf her. She closed her eyes, her heart unable to contain the happiness that surged through it in joyful torrents.

The building was like a dream. It seemed unreal, a thing of such overwhelming beauty that onlookers had to catch their breath. Manikottai was transformed yet again. It had gone from dark to light, from gloom to happiness. It sparkled like a jewel at the edge of the cliff, taking on the personality of its extraordinary owners. Landscaped gardens spralled into many tiers, overlooking the main structure. Fountains flowed with perfumed water in these gardens that were heavy with the intoxicating fragrance of frangipani. Little lamps hung like miniature moons all over the garden. Gleaming statues stood around, perfectly sculpted masterpieces of brass, stone, and marble. Mayilvilakkus that towered over six feet stood at every corner, casting dancing shadows with their flickering flames on the walls. Lotuses floated dreamily in silvery pools. The moonlight undulated over the terrace of the palace, bathing in its golden hue the two people entwined in each other's arms.

Mekalai looked up at her newly wedded husband. He shone like a star that night and his radiance scorched through his being. His skin was iridescent, gleaming like a polished gem.

'You goddess,' he murmured, burying his face in her glittering tresses. They stayed locked in embrace. They were interrupted by a meek voice. 'Your Majesty, the guests are waiting for you downstairs.'

Vikraman groaned. 'Tell them all to go away. I want to be alone with my bride...' The attendant stayed there, slightly perplexed.

Mekalai pulled his arm saying, 'Come, we must go down. These people want to see you, their new lord and master. Nithilan has invited practically the whole of Tamilakkam to his little sister's wedding.'

As they made their way down the colossal staircase, Vikraman asked, 'Is this a good time to tell them, you think, that I was the one who stole their riches?'

Mekalai laughed. 'No, that will only give them all heart attacks and ruin our wedding day for us!' She leaned closer into him, breathing in his masculine fragrance. 'Let that be our little secret,' she said, smiling.

He looked into her eyes and saw his world in it—a perfect world till the end of eternity. The thief of Poompuhar had finally managed to steal away his beloved. The universe seemed to fade and now all that mattered was their love...

A NOTE ON THE AUTHOR

Nila Iyer grew up at her ancestral home amidst the verdant serenity of Kerala's landscape. As a child, she loved to listen to her grandfather's stories about damsels, dragons, and princes on black stallions. By the time she was eighteen, she had devoured every romance novel at her disposal. Nila now lives in Mumbai and spends her days seeing her fantasies come alive on the imaginary pages on her laptop that she carries everywhere with her. A hit at parties, she is adept at conjuring up colourful and sometimes questionable love stories for her friends.

OTHER TITLES IN THE SERIES

Mistress to the Yuvraj
Sanyogita Rathore

Devastatingly handsome Rajput lothario Shivendra of Jaigarh has a formidable reputation—until he meets his match in bewitching Nandini, the headstrong daughter of an improverished zamindar from Multan. He decides he must have Nandini as his mistress, but she is determined to resist his indecent proposal, attracted as she is to him. Shivendra is persistent, however, and defies convention to bring them together illicitly. For how long, and to what end? Through desert sandstorms and Mughal camps, the epic love story of the yuvraj and his impetuous lover unfolds.

Ghazal in the Moonlight
Alessandra Shahbaz

Dazzling Shameena runs wild in the Nawab's palace in Lucknow until her weak-willed father promises her to Nicholas Winthrop, the richest Englishman in the subcontinent. Furious about the alliance, she rebels and flees her father's home, disguised as a courtesan. But when Asef, the thrillingly mysterious bodyguard of Nicholas, is dispatched to bring her back, Shameena finds herself caught in a dangerous game, between East and West, fire and ice...

The Zamindar's Forbidden Love
Jasmine Saigal

Madhubati, the beautiful, fiesty daughter of a Bengali teacher who tutors sons of rich zamindars, is pledged to Bidyut, the son of a family friend. But when fate brings her father's dashing student Som into her life, just as it did six years ago, the voluptuous village belle is forced to choose between fighting against their families—and against her fast-beating heart. Will love prevail over reason and class?

Passion in the Punjab
Kiran Kohl

Rani, a radiant Punjabi beauty and the illegitimate daughter of Maharajah Ranjit Singh, is kidnapped by the notorious bandit Ranbir .Singh, who decides to use her as a pawn in his revenge against the King. But soon she realizes she cannot ignore her desire for her captor, handsome and mysterious as he is. Torn between passion and loyalty, past and present, Rani must discover what really lies in her heart.